DEATH IN
DARKNESS

By the same author

as James Fraser

THE EVERGREEN DEATH
THE COCK-PIT OF ROSES
DEADLY NIGHTSHADE
DEATH IN A PHEASANT'S EYE
BLOOD ON A WIDOW'S CROSS
THE FIVE-LEAFED CLOVER
WREATH OF LORDS AND LADIES

as Alan White

THE LONG DAY'S DYING
THE WHEEL
THE LONG NIGHT'S WALK
THE LONG DROP
KIBBUTZ
THE LONG WATCH
THE LONG MIDNIGHT
CLIMATE OF REVOLT
THE LONG FUSE
THE LONG SUMMER

ARMSTRONG
DEATH IN DUPLICATE

Death in Darkness

an Armstrong novel

ALAN WHITE

COMMUNICA-EUROPA

First published in 1975 by
Barrie & Jenkins Ltd.
24 Highbury Crescent, London N5 1RX

Copyright © Alan White, 1975
ISBN 0 214 20180 5

All rights reserved.
No part of this publication
may be reproduced in any form or by any means
without the prior permission of Barrie & Jenkins Limited.

Printed in Great Britain by litho by The Anchor Press Ltd
and bound by Wm Brendon & Son Ltd
both of Tiptree, Essex

'Get into that hole,' he said, 'get right down.'

'*Why*, for God's sake *why* are you doing this to me?' the man asked. 'I can do nothing to help you.'

'You'd never understand, even if I told you. Life has always been good to you. How can you hope to understand men like me?'

'You know you won't get away with it!' Despite the fear he had earlier felt and not, he hoped, shown, now his voice was firm, almost tranquil, as if he'd come to terms with what was happening. The water swirled below him, dark, gleaming in continuous motion, almost attracting him. His feet were poised on a wide ledge which sloped downwards, curving round the inside of the bell-shaped cavern like an interior circular staircase. He'd always been afraid of holes and of the dark though that was something he'd told no one.

The boy with the shotgun was standing some distance away, the gun cradled beneath his arm, both barrels loaded. Ought he to have tried to take the gun? It would have been a foolish, almost naïve, gesture, no more. The boy looked as if he'd had experience of shotguns. Cold morning. Dew everywhere. That black water, in the hole, dominating all their thoughts.

'Go down,' the man said. 'There's no more time.'

At the last moment there should be time. There should be time, if only to prepare one's mind for the infinity of what was happening. No man should rush headlong into eternity.

'Fire the gun,' he said, but the boy shook his head, smiling.

He felt ashamed he'd revealed even that much of his fear.

So many questions he'd still like to ask. Not factual questions of 'why'. Questions about himself. Would he wait until the last minute? Would he crouch in this vast cavern, waiting until the very last moment, clinging to hope when hope had gone? Or would he take control of the moment of his own death, his own departure into whatever other life, if any, might be waiting? Would he let himself slip slowly down as the water rose, filling the cavern? Would he dive into its black and welcoming death? He no longer had any thoughts about the life he was leaving. Somehow, all that had been put out of his mind, all thoughts of what was to be in the future, what might have been, what could have been.

Suddenly his spirit rebelled. He turned and looked up at his captor, rage working on his face. 'You won't get away with it,' he shouted as his hands scrabbled at the edges of the hole, trying to lift his body out and clear. The boy with the shotgun moved forward, without urgency. The heavy stone slab slid sideways and he snatched his fingers away to prevent them being trapped by it. Then it thudded down, narrowly missing his head. It covered the hole completely, with only a narrow strip of light showing along one edge. He tried to push it upwards with his hands, but the effort was wasted. He knew he had no hope of lifting that stone. He went to the sloping wall of the cavernous hole, resting his back against the slime he remembered was green.

Then, quietly, he began to cry. . . .

CHAPTER ONE

I was sitting at my desk when the telephone rang. It had been one of those mornings, so far, and I wondered if I could survive until Emily came along the corridor with the coffee trolley. I'd been up half the previous night on a supermarket stake-out; we'd had a tip it was going to be raided and, despite my protests, the superintendent had insisted on a full alert. The tip-off came from one of Adams's lads and he was dead unreliable. They'd let us go home about five o'clock; I'd had three hours' sleep before leaving to come back to the Station.

Sarah had made me a breakfast I couldn't face. 'Don't tell me you're not well, too,' she said, then told me our daughter Helen had been up sick half the night and Sarah had made her stay in bed. When I arrived at the Station I found a pile of expenses forms the chief inspector had refused to sign. A shoplifter we were holding in the cells overnight, since he had no fixed address, had tried to hang himself with a rope knotted from his blanket; and I'd misplaced a forensic report I'd been asked to read and comment on, last thing last evening just before we took off for the stake-out.

I snatched up the telephone. 'Inspector Armstrong.'

'There's no need to shout, Inspector,' Sergeant Jones said, chuckling. He ran our front desk during office hours with considerable efficiency and never-failing good-humour, which wasn't bad considering that this time last year we were collecting round the office for a wreath and his wife was sorting out her black clothes. He was in the heavy mob in those days when they moved in on a gang having a go at the back door of a bank. The gang had beaten him with lead pipes; we thought he was dead when we put him in the ambulance. Now he had a silver plate where most people had a skull but apart from getting the occasional headache and dizziness he was normally as right as rain.

'A man down here,' he said, 'insists on talking to somebody. Normally I'd deal with it, but this one has a smell. . . .'

'Tell him to take a bath!'

'You know what I mean.'

Alas, I did know what he meant. Whatever they may say, police work is based on instinct, on having a 'nose' for a situation or a person that smells wrong. Inspector Adams, who normally occupied the desk across from mine, was in hospital because he didn't have that sense. He went in too close to a nice little old lady he found hanging about at the back of Woolworths. She stabbed him with a pair of stolen scissors. He's been in the Intensive Care Unit for thirty-six hours.

'What's his story?'

'He hasn't got one, yet. Said he'll talk to an officer, not a sergeant. Normally I'd handle him myself, you know that. But this one, I don't know.'

Listening to Sergeant Jones's Welsh lilt, I caught a whiff of the undertone of anxiety in his voice, and that surprised me. The sergeant doesn't get excited easily.

'What do you suggest?'

'Shall I put him in the interview room?'

'I'll be right down.'

Let me tell you about interview room one, since I was destined to spend a lot of time there that day. It's an idea we had in the Inspectors' Room and for once the chief listened to us. We see many people in the Station, not necessarily criminals, from whom we need a lot of information, a lot of cooperation. One of our chief difficulties is to get such people to relax, and it's even harder to do that in a bare-walled room containing only a desk and two chairs that reek of fear sweat. So, we reasoned, why not have a room that would put people at their ease. With a carpet on the floor, for example, to deaden some of the sound so that, everytime they said anything, their voices wouldn't bounce off the walls to accuse them. Comfortable chairs to sit on. Even a sofa, a couple of tables like you find in someone's home, not like prison office desks, a standard lamp instead of an overhead bare bulb, and even a television set in the corner. It wouldn't matter if it was hooked to an aerial or not, just so that the goggle eye would give the comfort of familiar surroundings.

To our great surprise, we got what we wanted. We were

even allowed to go round to a furnishing store and select it. Now we have an interview room that reminds people of home – a couple of deep moquette-covered armchairs and sofa to match, carpet on the floor, a TV and also a cassette player, with a few tapes, so we can turn on the soft lights and sweet music bit. And believe me, it works. There's even a bog and bathroom.

Of course, we still take the old lags into the cold empty places, sit them at the desk on a hard wood chair and, when necessary, shout at them.

I walked down the flight of stairs that brought me level with the entrance lobby, the desk across one far side where Sergeant Jones sat with his two constables. He nodded at me without speaking then beckoned with his head over his shoulder. The interview room was off this front lobby. I opened the door and went in.

A man was sitting in one of the armchairs and he got up when I came in. A policeman's eye is like the shutter of a polaroid camera. Takes instant snapshots, then prints a picture. At some time in the past, he's been banged about. Nose broken. Physical description: height five feet ten, weight eight/nine stones maximum, and there's not a lot of fat. At that weight, there's not a lot of anything. Hair dark, eyes brown and set very wide apart. Ears prominent, nose long and thin, slightly hooked. If you're lucky, the photograph is in three dimensions. You see the physical characteristics and the clothing and print out a few impressions. For example, this man didn't bother too much about himself. He combed his hair with his fingers, didn't wash it or himself too often. He was wearing a blue shirt that hadn't been ironed for a long time. His boots didn't fit, too wide and too long, and of course they hadn't been cleaned in a long time but that doesn't mean too much these days. Over the shirt a jacket that once had been a sports coat but now hung in loose folds from his pinched shoulders. Trousers too short and no trace of a crease. Okay, he was one of the unfortunates. You see them every day at the Labour Exchange – the Department of Employment as it's now grandly called. It's still the Labour Exchange to a lot of people. Quick look at his eyes. No sign of dilated pupils and his irises are clear.

'I'm Inspector Armstrong. They tell me you want to see an

officer. I'm an officer.'

When he spoke his voice put him at the centre of the grammar-school range. He articulated clearly, spoke correctly, and slowly enough for me to understand every word.

'I want you to understand, Inspector, that I'm not crazy. I want you to take me seriously. That's why I asked to see an officer. An officer, presumably, has time to take people seriously . . . ?'

Reasonable, rational, sincere. Age, it would be hard to say. Somewhere between forty and fifty? Job status – clerk in an office, shop assistant, draughtsman, salesman? No, not a salesman. He had none of the come-on.

'Would you like to sit down,' I said, 'and tell me your name?'

He sat in one of the chairs, slowly, carefully, a man protecting his bones from sudden shock. As he sat down he put his hands on the arms of the chair and I saw how they looked. Broken and knotted, like someone with terrible arthritis. He sat upright in the armchair, deliberately preventing himself from reclining back into it. We'd selected those chairs carefully, testing the furniture shop's whole range to find something that people could settle into without feeling they were lounging about. He sat bolt upright. A lot of people do at first, but then, gradually, they lean back. That's when we know we have their confidence. I hadn't got his, yet. But it was early.

'They call me Jim,' he said, 'but my name's really James. James Bishop. I live at number 5, Arlington Villas, just around the corner from here. In the basement.'

The area of London I work in tends to be high class. South of the Park, near Kensington High Street and all that. We have the Royal Hall on our patch, and a few millionaires' houses. We also have a few slums. Arlington Villas, despite its grand name, is one of the latter. Property developers have been after it for years, to pull it down and erect a skyscraper block, but there's a problem about titles. I don't see how they can ever resolve it unless the Council slaps a Compulsory Purchase Order on it. Meanwhile it's occupied by a disproportionate number of people, as many as ten or twelve to a house, all living in single rooms. Most of the women go out cleaning, most men do handyman jobs. It's a tired street of old houses gradually falling into total disrepair, but which refuse, thanks to their Victorian builders, to fall down. The occupants are like the houses, mostly old and shabby, coughing and wheezing and limping through a life that holds no obvious attractions, but all refusing to fall down.

I sat still.

'You can make notes if you want to,' he said.

He had an unusual self-confidence for a man of his social type. Almost as if he'd known better days in better places. Or as if he'd trained himself to it, refusing to be beaten. What was the motto we had in the Army —*nil illegitimus carborundum* — don't let the bastards grind you down.

'I'm taking notes in my head. I have a habit of losing scraps of paper.'

Let him relax. Don't push him, don't show on my face how many other things I have to do. I'd like to ring home, among other things, to ask about my daughter Helen, wondering what was wrong. It could be nothing. Perhaps something she'd eaten had disagreed with her. Young girls' stomachs are easily upset at that difficult stage of puberty. I'd like to ring Sarah to find out. I also thought I knew where I'd put that forensic report. There'd be hell to pay if it was really lost. I think I stuck it *under* my desk tray. I'd have to come to some agreement with the chief about those expense accounts. It was getting to be ridiculous. Either he accepted that I had the responsibility of checking them, that I would only sign them if I knew them to be authentic, and that his countersignature was a matter of form, or I'd pass them all up to him and let him check them. It was a waste of time, two of us checking a sergeant's claim for a measly quid for a taxi allowance, fifty pence for a meal, twenty pence for a drink for an informer.

Right. Enough time to relax. 'You wanted to see an officer, Mr Bishop. I'm an officer. What can I do for you?' None of this first-name stuff, not yet. Treat him to a bit of dignity. Poor bastard doesn't look as if he gets too much of that scarce commodity. Glance at my watch, just to show him we don't have all the time in the world, though he can have his fair share of it.

He laughed. It was a nervous bark, and he covered it by putting his hand over his face and rubbing it. Again I saw the knuckles. If that was arthritis, poor bugger! If it was something else – an industrial accident, for example. . . ? I once saw a man who'd got his hands caught in a lathe. They looked something like that when the surgeons had finished putting his bones together again.

'I want a million pounds,' he said.

Just like that. A million pounds. So, he's another nutter. We get them all the time. That makes life easy. I can cope with nutters. It's men with real problems who take up your time.

'A million pounds, eh? And what makes you think I have a million pounds to give you?'

'I don't think *you* have a million pounds. But I think you can speak to the people who do have. Like the Bank of England.'

'And what makes you think I'm going to talk to them?' Stay loose, as they say nowadays. Play it cool. Nutters can be violent.

A button had been built into the arm of each chair. Under the fabric. Impossible to find if you don't know where it is. Pressing the button once lights the desk sergeant's telephone console. Pressing the button twice makes the light blink on and off, on and off. One press.

There was a knock on the door. 'Come in,' I said. Before the door could open, James Bishop was standing up. He could move fast. The door opened and the sergeant came in. Behind him I could see Constable Arkwright. Standard procedure. 'You're wanted on the telephone, Inspector.'

'Thank you, Sergeant.' Turn to Bishop, smile. 'Won't keep you a minute.' Arkwright in through the door, gently. Stands there. It's a rotten job. 'Ah, Constable Arkwright . . .' as if he carried the Holy Grail. 'Just keep Mr Bishop company for a few minutes while I answer the telephone, will you?' Walk slowly towards the door, keeping my heart from thumping. This is the moment they pull out the gun, the knife, the razor. This is the moment they jump, screaming and scratching like wild cats. Because they know, they know they're being manoeuvred.

Sergeant Jones moves forward, a technique from his rugby days, to cover my back. He won't be much good, nowadays. The first sign of violence and he gets a dizzy spell. You can't blame the poor sod. Everybody knows it's psychosomatic, but if you've ever gone down while four tough bastards beat at you with lead pipes. . . .

But no problems. Bishop stands there, still as a statue.

I get to the door. Turn. Standard smile on my face, not overdone. 'Shan't be a moment.' That's a lie and I can see he knows it and I know it.

'Take your time, Inspector. I'll wait.'

Dammit, I know he'll wait.

I went out and Sergeant Jones followed me, leaving Arkwright in there, on his own. Like I said, it's a rotten job, not knowing.

'What's the problem?' Sergeant Jones asked.

'A nutter. Asked me for a million pounds . . .'

'He'll be lucky. On your pay . . .'

'Told me I could get it from the Bank of England. That's a laugh. I've got the best bank manager in the world but the way things are, he has to give me the third degree before he can lend me a fiver.'

I went back upstairs. Standard procedure. We have a Book of Rules that tells us how to do everything. Of course I don't always follow it and that's given me a reputation. But I can live with that. The Book of Rules said I had to go back to my office, back to my daily routine. Constable Arkwright would stay in the interview room with Mr Bishop. Sergeant Jones would go about *his* business for ten minutes, perhaps a little longer, then he'd go back into the interview room, give Mr Bishop my apologies and say I'd been called out on an urgent matter. If Mr Bishop would care to come back in the morning. . . ? If Mr Bishop asked for another 'officer' Sergeant Jones had the standard answer. Inspector Armstrong had taken Mr Bishop's preliminary statement, and an officer always liked to follow through his own cases. Anyway, there was no other officer in the building. Meanwhile, if Mr Bishop would care to come back in the morning. . . . All very polite.

They seldom returned. If they did, the officer concerned was temporarily out of the building. If they'd care to come back the following day . . .

You may think we're a cruel lot of bastards, but we do honestly try to help when we can. Even nutters. A copper spends half his life just providing an ear for somebody. Just listening. I don't mind. I'm old-fashioned enough to believe that's what the police force is supposed to do. That and crime prevention.

It isn't a popular point of view on an understaffed force, when my colleagues are chasing about like blue-arsed flies and I'm sitting down saying yes dear no dear to some old spinster who just wants to talk to somebody, talk to anybody, before she goes back to her cold flat and her cat and the shared tin of sardines.

I used the ten minutes' waiting period to ring Sarah.

'I don't like the look of Helen,' she said. 'I've asked Doctor James to come round. He should be here soon.'

'What do *you* think it is?'

'I don't know. She was sick all night. I thought it might be a touch of food poisoning.'

'What did she have for supper?'

'A poached egg on toast. . . .'

'No harm in that.'

'Ah, yes, but she went out for half an hour. You know how she goes to the fish-and-chip shop sometimes. She said she hadn't, but I'm not so sure. . . .' She switched abruptly, guessing, I suppose, that I didn't have much time. I never did when I called from the office. 'Nancy was on the telephone,' she said. 'I can't see why you bother.'

Nancy was a young widow, lived in the street behind us. She'd been left with a son, a young rip of fourteen, when her husband was killed in a car smash. He was a rep., travelling about all over the country, often away. The lad had got out of control. I used to talk to him sometimes when he needed the riot act reading to him. Nancy thought it came better from a policeman. Sarah said Nancy fancied me. It was hard to explain I was only trying to help, and that Nancy and I didn't huddle on the sofa every time I went round there.

'What is it this time?'

'That lad of hers. . . .'

'He's got a name. . . .'

'I know what name I'd like to call him. . . .'

'Don't be vindictive, Sarah. Count your blessings he's not one of ours. . . .'

'I know what I'd do with him, if he was. . . .'

'What about him, Sarah? I haven't much time.'

'He's still in bed. Won't get up. Says he's not going to school any more. How do you like that. A fourteen-year-old boy telling his mother he's not going to school any more. . . .'

'Ring me when the doctor's been,' I said, and hung up.

Then I rang Nancy's number.

'Put him on the phone,' I said.

'He won't come if he knows it's you.'

'Then tell him it's some girl.'

I could hear her shout. 'Stephen. Telephone. . . . I don't know, it's some girl. . . .'

Pause. Then the phone being picked up. 'Hello, Judy . . .?'

'It's not Judy, you little bastard. It's Mr Armstrong. Put your clothes on and go to school, or I'll detail a couple of constables to come and take you, and put some clothes on because they'll drag you there, even if you're in your underpants.'

There are times to be tough with kids his age. This was one of them. Nancy's problem was that she didn't know how. I did. I'd trained in a hard school.

'I don't feel well. . . .'

Now he was whining, but I'd heard him do that before and wasn't impressed, not this time. I had to take a chance.

'Listen to me, Stephen. You know well enough by now that I don't say anything I don't mean. Put your clothes on and go to school. If you don't feel well, tell the teacher when you get there. If you don't do that right away, I'll send two constables to take you. The Law against truancy says you have to go to school and I'm in a position to see the Law is obeyed. So, put your clothes on and off you go to school!'

What a way to start a day.

I heard the coffee trolley rattling down the corridor. Thank God for that. I was going outside to get a cup when the phone went again. It was Sergeant Jones.

'We've got a right one here, Inspector,' he said. 'He won't leave. Said he'll wait until you come back, whatever time that may be. Settled back into the armchair as if he owned it. . . .'

'Oh, hell, Sergeant. I've got a million things to do.'

'So have I, Inspector.'

'You couldn't just tell Arkwright to chuck him out?'

'Normally I would. But this one. . . . Somehow, I've got . . .'

'. . . a smell about him. I know. Okay, I'll come down.'

Some things you ignore in the hope they'll go away. Like a

blinding headache, a pain in your tooth, a tax assessment. Some of them never go away. Like James – they call me Jim – Bishop.

I went into the interview room all smiles. 'Sorry to keep you,' I said, making no reference to the fact that they'd tried to get rid of him and failed.

'That's all right,' he said; then, cheeky bugger, added, 'I know how busy you must be.'

How do you approach a man like this? There was no starting point, no frame of reference.

'Why do you think I'm going to provide you with a million pounds?' I asked. I had to start somewhere.

He nodded, satisfied that now we were back on the track.

'Because I've kidnapped Prince Charles,' he said. 'I've got him hidden away where you'll never find him, and if you don't give me a million pounds, I shall leave him where he is and he'll die. Within eight hours.'

Oh my God, oh my merciful God in Heaven above. This one was a right nutter. A million pounds . . . kidnapped Prince Charles . . . die within eight hours. Book of Rules, mentally flick it open to page thirty-eight. 'Any mention of Royals must be referred to an officer of the rank of chief inspector and above.' Then a list. Prince Charles was second on that list. No prize for guessing who was at the top.

I picked up the telephone. It's one of the modern ones and I dropped it, trying to dial the internal number. James Bishop was smiling, obviously enjoying himself enormously. He was beginning to get on my wick. Okay, you bastard, this one we'll try straight down the line. Wipe that smirk off your face.

'Chief Inspector? Armstrong here. I'm with a man in interview room one. He's asked me for a million pounds. Says he's kidnapped Prince Charles and has him hidden. He also says that, if he doesn't get the money, Prince Charles will die in eight hours. . . .'

'*Within* eight hours,' Bishop said, interrupting me.

'Sorry, *within* eight hours.'

'What's he like? Round the bend?'

'Yes.'

'Why bother me? Throw him out.'

One up for me. 'I was thinking, Chief, of page thirty-eight.'

'Ah yes, referral to a superior officer. Quite right, Inspector. I'll come down. But warn Sergeant . . . Jones, is it today . . . ?'

'Jones, Chief.'

While he was talking, I had pressed the button twice. That would put on a winking light on the sergeant's console. He'd know what to do, but wait until the light held steady. Then the heavies would come in, fast.

'The chief inspector is coming down,' I said to Bishop. 'You have two alternatives. Either you can leave now, quietly, and we'll forget all about this, or you can wait until the chief has seen you. He'll either book you with interfering with the police in the execution of their duties, or he'll have you thrown out. It's up to you. When you mentioned Prince Charles's name, you took the whole matter out of my hands.'

'Bureaucracy, eh?'

'I don't have the clout to deal with Royal Personages. Come on, why don't you scarper, quick, before the chief gets here? I can tell you privately, he's a right bastard. Especially when he thinks he's having his leg pulled.'

'I think I'll wait,' he said.

It took the chief only a couple of minutes. 'Kidnapped Prince Charles, have you?' he barked without waiting for an introduction. 'What about his private detective. You kidnapped him, too?'

Bishop was smiling. Now that the inspector was carrying the interview, I had a chance to watch Bishop in action.

'That would be telling, wouldn't it?' he said.

'Where've you got him hidden, eh?'

Bishop sighed. 'You don't imagine I'm going to tell you *that* do you?'

'This million pounds. Where are we going to get it?'

'I imagine from the Bank of England, but I don't care.'

The chief inspector leered. 'Have you any idea, my good man, just what a million pounds *looks* like? What it weighs?'

'Yes, I have. It's fifty thousand twenty pound notes. Done up a thousand to a bundle, that takes fifty bundles. It will fit into a large suitcase.'

'Got it all worked out, have you?'

I squirmed, seeing the look on Bishop's face, his blatant contempt for the chief's sarcasm. To my way of thinking, the chief was losing this round badly. He'd started it badly by coming in too hard and too fast. Now that I could observe him, I could see that Bishop was stronger than I'd thought.

'Of course I've got it all worked out. You don't think I'd come in here *until* I'd worked it out, do you?'

Again, that inner strength. Whatever Bishop may be, he was no mug to be browbeaten. He'd need more careful handling than the chief inspector was giving him. I coughed. The chief turned round and glared at me. I don't think he enjoyed my seeing him done down.

'Should we telephone the Palace, perhaps?' I asked, diffidently.

The chief picked up the telephone. 'Send someone in with Ops 4 for today,' he said, looking at me.

Ops 4 was a daily sheet, gave a list of the extraordinary movements on our patch for the twenty-four hours from midnight. I ought to have thought of that. Sergeant Jones brought it in himself and gave it to the chief. I'd glanced at it briefly when I had arrived for work. I seemed to remember that Princess Margaret was attending a function in the Royal Hall this afternoon, Prince Philip was speaking at the Park Royal Hotel this evening, but no mention of Prince Charles.

Bishop spoke, his voice quietly amused. 'Prince Charles is supposed to be having a day off today,' he said. 'He's gone sailing. With Lord Wentworth. On *The Song Bird*.'

Each of us looked at him. I suppose that was the moment at which I started to believe he might not be a nutter; perhaps, after all, he might be telling the truth.

'How the devil did you know that?' the chief asked, his eyes staring.

Sergeant Jones had been thinking. 'He could have read it, chief, in some gossip column. Perhaps that's what provoked him to come up here and tell us a cock-and-bull story.'

It was a good guess. He couldn't have known Bishop had told us he'd kidnapped Prince Charles. But it was a safe bet, knowing that Bishop had asked for a million.

'I can give you a timetable,' Bishop said quietly.

The chief had picked up the telephone. 'Get me a call on

the red Z line,' he said. It was put through immediately. 'Chief Inspector Roberts here,' he said, then a short list of letters and numbers. They'd be checking, identifying him. 'Prince Charles?' he asked. He could equally well have said another code number, but I guess he was shaken. He paused, then said thank you and put down the telephone. I wished I were playing poker against him for a large stake. We could all read his hand, including Bishop. We all knew the prince had taken a day off his official duties to go sailing. Possibly with Lord Wentworth. They often sailed together, as anybody who reads the newspapers must know.

'He *could* have read it in a gossip column,' Sergeant Jones said, his Welsh stubbornness sounding in his voice. 'Let me check, Chief Inspector?' The chief nodded.

The sergeant picked up the telephone, asked for an outside line, dialled a number. When they put him through, he asked for someone called Wally. Wally came on the line, his voice booming so loud we could hear it, though not make out the words. 'You read the gossip columns, Wally,' Sergeant Jones said after identifying himself. 'Can you give me a reference to a mention of Prince Charles going sailing with Lord Wentworth?'

Whoever 'Wally' was, he knew the newspapers intimately. Quickly he rattled off three names, three dates. *Evening Standard* last Tuesday, *Daily Mail* this morning, Jennifer's Diary in *The Tatler* out yesterday. The sergeant put down the telephone, a satisfied smile on his face. 'Three newspapers have quoted the fact that the prince was going sailing with Lord Wentworth,' he said. 'Mr Bishop could have read any of them, though I don't imagine he's one of Jennifer's regular readers . . .' Both of them laughed, the tension broken. Me, I was a bit more sceptical.

'Throw him out,' the chief inspector said. The door opened, and Arkwright and Milton came in. Both are well over standard height and standard weight. Milton is in the divisional boxing team, and looks it. Bishop came out of the chair, fast.

'Why don't you go back to Arlington Villas, Mr Bishop,' I said. 'Make yourself a cup of tea?'

His upper lip curled back from his teeth in an animal snarl. 'Come on,' I said, 'I'll walk back with you. . . .'

I walked across the room towards him with my hand held out, but he crouched back towards the wall, his face still wearing that expression. Now I could believe he was mentally unbalanced. He looked insane. Or terrified. 'I won't go,' he said, 'and you can't make me.'

'Come on lads,' Sergeant Jones said, 'let's make it quick. We'll take him out the back door.'

Looking at Bishop I knew they wouldn't be able to 'make it quick'. Somebody, most probably Bishop, would get hurt. He'd hang on to every piece of furniture, every door, every corner. Now his body was arched forwards in an inexpert imitation of a boxer's stance. Milton would get under and in with no difficulty. He could trap Bishop's arms, Arkwright could get his legs, and they could lift him out of the station. We get used to it, the number of demonstrators we have to deal with these days, the number of people we have to pick up off the pavements. Most of them aren't as thin and emaciated as Bishop though. Most of them, despite the placards that tell the rest of us that we're robbing them, seem to have had enough food to make them strong, enough food to make a copper's job a nightmare.

'Hang on!' I said. I turned to the chief. 'Could I have ten minutes with him, Chief?' I asked. 'Just ten minutes alone with him?'

'To do what?'

I have a reputation as a thumper, a man who hits first and asks the questions later. Nothing could be further from the truth. I have recognized there are times you have to move like lightning, when you can't take the time for the niceties of understanding. You have to hit hard and fast. If Adams had hit that sweet little old lady hard and fast he wouldn't be in the Intensive Care Unit right now, battling for life with a scissor wound in his belly.

'I just want to talk to Mr Bishop. Quietly.'

The chief shrugged his shoulders. 'Whenever you get a case, Inspector, things seem to become complicated. This man has nothing but a cock-and-bull story. He's wasting our and your time. Get rid of him, as quickly as you can.'

I could see he didn't like the idea of me being left alone

with Bishop. He thought that by devoting an inspector's time to him, we were according Bishop more importance that he merited. But Bishop was a human being in distress and I'm enough of a sucker to fall for that. It gets me into a lot of trouble at work and at home but it's my nature and there appears to be nothing I can do to change that. Basically, I don't think I want to.

'Give him ten minutes,' the chief said, 'and I shall want to see you in my office afterwards.' He didn't trust me to make it only ten minutes. He and the sergeant followed the two constables out. Bishop was still against the wall, staring at me like a cat willing itself to spring, crouched in an attitude of hatred.

'Take it easy, Mr Bishop,' I said. 'Nobody's going to hurt you, so you might as well sit down.'

He stayed where he was but his attitude seemed to change and I could see some of the tension begin to leave him. I sat in one of the chairs. The telephone was on a table beside it. I picked it up. 'Get us a couple of cups of coffee,' I said. The switchboard girl started to give me an argument. 'Look, I know the trolley's going round. I missed it upstairs. But I want a couple of cups of coffee in interview room one, quick.' She gave me another argument and I nearly lost my temper. I severed the connection, dialled the desk number. 'Get me a couple of cups of coffee in here, Sergeant,' I said. 'The switchboard girl's giving me an argument and I haven't the time . . . I *know* she's just obeying the rules . . . I don't care. Send a constable out to Joe Lyons. . . .'

'Bloody bureaucracy,' I said.

I think that relaxed Bishop more than anything else I could have said. He stood more straight, slowly let those terrible hands go down his sides.

'What have you done to your hands?' I asked him.

'Don't bother making conversation. And don't think that in ten minutes you're going to change my story. I've kidnapped Prince Charles, I've hidden him away, and he'll die in eight hours unless I walk out of here with a million pounds.'

'You said "within eight hours" before. Which is it? In or within?' It would have to be "in", wouldn't it? If it was within, well, "now" was "within" wasn't it, and by that reckoning

Prince Charles could already be dead.

'All right. *In* eight hours.'

Words are important when you're interviewing. Single words can reveal a lot to you. If Bishop were serious, 'in' eight hours would suggest a time factor, and that would mean a timing mechanism. If we were looking for something, eventually, it would help to know what we were looking for. I was surprised by my own thinking. Had I accepted his story? I wasn't aware of having changed my point of view. So far as I was concerned, Bishop was a nutter and my only reason for talking to him was to prevent him being damaged inadvertently when they carried him out and dumped him in the back yard.

'You seem a rational sort of man,' I said. It was true. Though what he was saying was utterly irrational, he seemed to be saying it with some sense of order. And not a madman's obsession.

'When you thought of coming in here, you must have guessed we wouldn't believe you. If this were the script of a film, you'd have brought something with you to convince us. A tape recording of his voice, for example, the clothes the prince was wearing. What *was* he wearing, by the way, when you kidnapped him?'

'A grey lounge suit.'

'I can check that, you know?'

'I know you can.'

'What time did you kidnap him?'

He wasn't going to answer that one! He walked across and sat in the armchair, relaxed again. He sat back all the way pressing those gnarled fingers together like the twigs of a figtree, curling round each other.

'And what about his detective? He always has a detective with him. Have you kidnapped the detective, too? Incidentally, for you to have kidnapped them and be here by this time of day you must have done it very early. Of course, if the prince were going sailing, he *would* get up very early. But you'd have to get your skates on to kidnap them, take them somewhere and hide them, and get back here by ten o'clock. You must have done the job about six, seven o'clock. That means you'd have to plan it ahead. That'd be difficult. People don't usually decide to go sailing until they can be certain what the weather is going to be like. What was the weather like, at six o'clock?'

'A good try, Inspector. Now you're playing at being a detective again, aren't you. . . .'

'Damn it, James, I *am* a detective.'

'The prince was going sailing for the day. With Lord Wentworth. He'd have a long way to travel, wouldn't he? He'd need to get up early to get there. Nobody starts a day's sailing at midday.'

'Where was he going?'

'To Chatham. The boat's in the Medway. They wanted to catch the tide.'

'I can check that business about Lord Wentworth's yacht being in the Medway, you know.'

'I know. I knew I was going to give you facts you could check. Facts you *would* check. I don't expect you to give me a million pounds for nothing.'

'But you *do* expect me to give you million pounds?'

'Eventually.'

'What about getting away with your million? What do we do, fly you somewhere? Put a plane at your disposal? You can't get away, you know. Not with a million pounds. We could seal off every airport. The minute you accept that money you've committed a crime for which we can chase you from here to Kingdom Come. Believe me, we will.'

The bastard smiled at me. I had to admire his guts.

'Nothing so elaborate and melodramatic as that. You give me a million pounds and I walk out of here. Only when I'm absolutely convinced that no one is following me, that nobody knows where I am, do I ring you to tell you where the prince is. The beauty of that is that you don't know where I'll be ringing from. You might have been able to trace the call in the old days, but now, with direct dialling, you don't stand much of a chance.'

'You seem to have worked it all out.'

'I like the simple approach. Life is too damned complicated, these days, too hemmed in with so-called sophistication.'

'There's nothing "unsophisticated" about a million pounds.'

'It's only a convenient sum of money. Enough to free me from all those people who keep brandishing rule books at me.'

I knew something of what he meant; nowhere is the rule book more frequently consulted than on the police force, and I'd acquired something of a reputation for being a man who preferred to act first, and look it up in the book later. I believe that rules are written for the guidance of people who don't know how to think for themselves. Rules are meant to be a starting point; often they become the end product.

'Had a lot of trouble with "rules", have you?'

He gave a hollow laugh. 'You'd be astounded If I told you,' he said, 'some of the games people play when they write the regulations. I read in the paper recently, a man working on the one-way system in Kensington designed all the streets and the flow of traffic in such a way that you could get in, but then there was no way you could get out. The Civil Service does it the opposite way. They make the rules so that they can get out of anything, but the outsider just can't get in. As you may have guessed, I'm an outsider. I always have been. Now, I intend to become an insider. That's what the million pounds will do. It'll help me tear up all the rule books.'

'If you get it. . . .'

'I will. You'll give it to me. The life of Prince Charles is something you can't equate with monetary terms. A company chairman, a politician, the child of a rich man, yes. But not the future king of this country.'

Again, that logic. That reasoned thinking. I'm not saying he was right in his conclusions, but he had thought it out. It would become a challenge. If he were to walk out of the door with a million pounds we'd keep a surveillance on him from every rooftop we could find. We'd use all the techniques we possess and he must know they are considerable. But in the face of his simple declaration, 'I won't telephone you until I can be certain I am not being followed', and with the life of the prince at stake, I knew damned well, and he knew too, we'd be powerless.

God knows what kind of a set up he'd made for himself. With a million pounds at his disposal, he could have made some impressive arrangements to get himself far away fast. Private plane, private boat. We *can't* check them all. Apart from anything else, God knows what kind of an identity he'd obtained for himself. It's not so difficult to get a phoney passport or to change your appearance sufficiently to fool an immigration official. Heathrow, Gatwick, Luton, Birmingham; Christ, the number of airports from which he could take off on a scheduled or a charter flight. He could leave the country as a businessman, or a tourist going for a holiday.

'I can't do it, you know,' I said to him. 'Be reasonable. I can't set the machinery in motion to get you a million pounds in cash within eight hours. . . .'

'It's seven hours now,' he reminded me gently. 'And in an hour from now, it will be six. In seven hours from now we'll have no option. Prince Charles will be dead. You'll never find him. You won't be able to charge me with his murder because you'll have no evidence. That's one of the reasons I didn't bring his clothing, a snip of his hair, a tape recording of his voice. So that you'd have no evidence with which to charge me.'

'For a man who lives in a basement room in Arlington Villas, you're not short of self-confidence,' I said sourly.

That nettled him. He stuck out his hands. 'You asked me about my hands,' he said, shaking them as if they were a couple of rag puppets. 'I haven't always lived in Arlington Villas. For two years I lived in a hole in the ground. I was a young man then, and believed in people like Prince Charles. King and Country. Rule Britannia.'

Quick calculation. He's younger than he looks, or should I say he looks older than his age because of his way of life, because he's suffered. 'Korea?'

He nodded. 'I was one of the ones they captured. They taught me many things. Oddly enough, without meaning to, they gave me self-confidence. I stayed alive whatever they did to me. I became confident I could always stay alive. If you can call it "living" in Arlington Villas, one room in the basement: another hole in the ground only this one lined with bricks instead of bamboo stakes. . . .'

What do you say to somebody at moments like this? Ex-prisoners-of-war keep cropping up, losing the battle to live normally again in a normal civilization. The last world war, the Korean war, the Vietnam war – though we don't get many of them except Americans who don't want to go back home.

'Let me walk home with you,' I said. 'You don't want to hang about this place. A police station is for criminals, lads who've dipped their hands in somebody else's pocket, mugs like that. . . .'

'You still don't believe me, do you?'

'No, I'm sorry but I don't. I just can't imagine it. Prince Charles is a biggish fellow. He's not one of the pampered weaklings. He's tough. And he has with him a detective who's not only tough, but well trained. You wouldn't stand a chance with either of them. They're both used to people trying to con them, to get close to them. Then again, there's the question of the money. A million pounds is too much for somebody like you to handle. No, I just can't see it.'

I had a sudden thought. 'Tell you what; I know a lady who has a nice house. Plenty of room in it. She was saying to me only the other day that she'd like to have a man about the place, to help her fix things when they go wrong. Her husband died and left her with a fourteen-year-old boy. He'd be better off with a man about the place. She's not short of money; her husband left her well provided for though she's not rich. If you'll come with me, now, we'll go to see her. If you both get on together, I'm sure she'll offer you the spare room and your keep if you're prepared to give a helping hand about the place. There's even a big garden if you like gardening. . . .'

He wasn't taking any interest in what I was saying. You know how it is when somebody is letting you rabbit on, waiting until your lips stop moving, not hearing what you're saying, not even listening. He was shaking his head.

'I knew it would be difficult to persuade you people,' he said, 'but I didn't know you'd be this stupid. Look, Inspector Armstrong, *I have kidnapped Prince Charles*. Can't you understand that? *I want a million pounds' ransom for him*. Isn't that clear? If I don't get it within eight hours, *Prince Charles will die*. You're a police officer. You should know what to do. So, for God's sake, do it.'

He was calm but emphatic, cold, clear, and rational. But what he was saying was so monstrous, so unbelievable.

'Oh, come on,' I said, rattled, 'piss off out of it. Go on, piss off.'

I got up, walked to the door and flung it wide open. He watched me with amused eyes but didn't move. I strode back across the room, reached out and grabbed his jacket lapels, and pulled him to his feet. He came up without a murmur, a loose sack of flesh and bones offering no resistance. With my other hand I grabbed his shoulder and propelled him towards the door. 'Go on, you silly bugger, piss off,' I said, angry with myself, angry with him, angry with the whole miserable existence, the whole modern world that had brought this man to such a situation.

I could rationalize it many ways. He was bored and wanted someone to talk to; he was oppressed and depressed, wanted for a few minutes to be the centre of any kind of activity to call attention to himself. Wanted, perhaps, no more than somebody to talk to. But he'd come in here with a ridiculous story that contained the seed of danger to himself. He wasn't like the old man who comes in regularly every month to tell us that somebody is tapping on his window every night trying to get in and rob him of the vast quantity of jewels he keeps beneath his bed. For old Harry we have a standard routine. Whoever happens to be the rookie on the desk is instructed to take him down to the canteen, buy him a cup of tea and a bun, and write a complete list of the jewels. Afterwards, old Harry leaves quiet as a mouse, happy for at least another month. Mister bloody Bishop wasn't like that.

When he got to the door he reached out his hand and held the door jamb. I pushed and nothing happened. I'd need to push really hard to get his hand off. It wouldn't be difficult; one chop on that bony emaciated wizened wrist and his hand would drop away from the door jamb. I couldn't bring myself to do it. Looking at that horrible hand I knew that too many people had chopped at it, too many blows had been directed towards it. I couldn't add mine. I let go of his shoulder. Put my arm round him.

'Mr Bishop, I'm asking you, sincerely, to go home. If you stay here and persist in this ridiculous story, we shall have to take some kind of action against you. We shall have to lock you up. That means I'll have to bring those two constables and they'll carry you down into the cells. You'll get hurt, bound to. I don't want that. Believe me, I don't want that. You've been hurt enough already. Whatever you may think, we're not sadists. We don't like to hurt people unnecessarily. So please,

please, won't you let me walk home with you, quietly, just the two of us. And make us a cup of tea, and we'll have a chat, and talk about things in general, in your own home, away from here and the officialdom. Here, Mr Bishop, I have to be a policeman. Outside, I can take my choice and try to be a human being.'

I thought I had him. I took my hand away from his shoulder. I thought he was going to say, 'All right, let's go.' He turned to look at me. I turned, too, looked back at the chair to make sure he hadn't left anything. I turned back, and already he was moving, back towards the chair, back towards his seat. He sat down, but I no longer cared. Or told myself I didn't care. I'd tried hard. If he wanted it the other way, that was his affair. I reached over and pressed the button twice. The sergeant came along the corridor with Arkwright and Milton.

'Throw him out,' I said, and went out of the room, back up the stairs to my office.

I sat at my desk, unaccountably shaken. After all it was routine. It wasn't the first time it had happened. That's why we'd had the buttons installed, damn it, so we could get rid of people quickly. We're supposed to uphold the Law, not act as an ear to every nut loose on the streets of London. Half the people in London, it sometimes seems to me, are out of their minds.

My hand shook a little as I reached for the telephone and dialled the chief's number.

'I've instructed them to throw him out,' I said.

'Good man. No sense in getting involved in a situation like that. He needs medical care and we haven't time to be psychiatrists. . . .'

'If we're not careful this could become a home from home for every nut north of the river.'

'That's right. I've been thinking about that supermarket tip-off. It could be he got the date wrong. Would you like to go and see him again?'

I groaned inwardly. 'Smithy is very unreliable, Chief,' I said. 'A couple of years back he tried it out on me but I never got a thing from him worth a damn. Adams is a mug to listen to him. How is he, by the way? Has anybody talked to the hospital?'

'I rang them half an hour ago. There's no change. Scissors

make an awful mess.'

'We ought to think about a collection.'

'Don't be a pessimist, Armstrong. He'll pull through. Adams is a tough lad. He has a lot of ambition and a lot to live for.'

That fellow, probably sprawled in the backyard by now, once had a lot to live for until they stuck him into a bamboo pit. I couldn't get him out of my mind.

I looked under the In-tray on my desk. Sure enough the forensic report was there. I read it again. A husband claimed his wife had been helping put up a pelmet for a curtain rail. The hammer, so he said, had dropped and hit her on the head. She died instantly. The autopsy showed she had a thin skull. Theoretically it was possible that a hammer dropping like that could have killed her, but I talked with her husband and got what Sergeant Jones would have called a 'smell' from him. I went back to the pathologist and asked him to do some tests. He practically rebuilt the skull and in doing so managed to prove to my satisfaction that the hammer blow had struck her at right angles to the back of her head. Back to the husband to talk with him.

'It must have been a terrible shock for you,' I said, 'standing up on top of a ladder with your wife down below looking up at you and suddenly dropping the hammer like that.'

He was suspicious of course, and clever, but not clever enough. 'Oh, she wasn't looking up at me,' he said.

'Where was she looking?'

'She was looking at the curtain, of course.'

Wrong answer. For the hammer to have done her the injury it did she'd have had to be looking at the ground. I was convinced he'd swung the hammer at her but how could I prove it. There was nothing to go on other than the 'smell' and the pathologist's report. If we tried to take it to court he could change his story and say she was looking down at the ground. The report established, unfortunately, that the woman *could* have been killed by a blow from that hammer falling six feet. The windows of their house were high, and standing on top of the ladder with his arms outstretched – and I got him to do that for me – the hammer would have been just more than six feet from her head. It was a tricky one and he didn't look the type to suffer remorse and confess. You can never tell. More than fifty per cent of all murders are never solved until the murderer walks in years later and says, 'I can't sleep at night thinking about it. I did it.' He didn't look the type.

I telephoned to the detective room, got Joseph Telfer. 'Joe,' I said, 'I want you to sniff about a bit on that Benton job. Ask around, find out if he's got a bird. I'm damn sure he killed his missus. You might also find out if there's an insurance policy, though he'd be a mug to try to collect insurance with a hammer.'

'Shall I tell Superintendent Bowkes?'

'Not yet.'

Bowkes was a rule book man. He'd insist on pulling Benton in for more grilling, but for the time being I'd be happier letting Benton stew in his own juice.

I put the phone down, sat staring at the expense accounts. Bishop would probably be home by now. Poor devil, probably find he had tea but no milk and sugar. Never mind, he might have a kind landlady who'd give him a brew-up. I hoped Milton hadn't hurt him too much. He doesn't know his own strength.

I pushed thoughts of Bishop to the back of my mind and rang Nancy. 'Has he gone to school?' I asked.

'He left here but I don't know where he's gone.'

'If I find he's played hookie I'll crucify him.'

'It's good of you to take the interest, Bill,' she said. 'You're very kind to us. I can't think why. I don't know how to repay you sometimes.'

There it was. The suggestion that perhaps there *was* something Nancy could do for me. In bed. Of course, I'd never take advantage of that, but it was there and Sarah knew it.

'Hey,' I said, 'I've got an idea for you. I may have found somebody to live in that spare room of yours. You always said you could do with a man about the house. I shouldn't think he's got any money though.'

I could sense the interest in her voice when she spoke. 'What's he like? I hope he won't be tapping on my bedroom door.' Randy bitch. That was just what she did hope. Maybe the two of them could make a go of it, who knows? Kill two birds with one stone. Get both of them off my back. I laughed, my good humour restored. Dammit, now I was playing cupid. Good old fix-'em-up Armstrong, that was me. In a couple of days I'd go round to Arlington Villas, see Bishop, fix him up with Nancy. I chuckled. 'That's a dirty laugh,' she said. 'You better not tell me what you're thinking. You might make me blush.'

'Blush, you? That'll be the day. . . .'

The phone rang as I put it down. 'You'll never guess who's walked in the front door again,' Sergeant Jones said. I groaned. 'Have Milton take him down to the canteen,' I said, 'buy him a cup of tea, then put him back in the interview room.'

'Shall I switch on the television?'

'Cheeky bugger. On second thoughts, why not? And while you're about it, make up the bed in there. I think we've got a lodger.'

CHAPTER TWO

I picked up the telephone and dialled a number.

A voice answered: 'Palace.'

I gave the chief inspector's string of numbers. He'd skin me alive if he knew. 'Prince Charles?' I said.

'This is the fourth call this morning. What's happening all of a sudden? He's gone sailing, taken a day off with Lord Wentworth.'

'Have you spoken with his detective?'

'No, we haven't, and we wouldn't expect to. There is no reason for us to speak with him.'

Service at the Palace had affected his style and manner of speaking. He sounded imperial, which had the effect of making me feel coarse.

'Keep your bloody shirt on,' I said, 'I'm just doing a job.'

'A hysterical woman from Surbiton has spotted Prince Charles's car being chased by a large black limousine full of men wearing dark hats. Someone in Leicestershire has telephoned to say that a horse has bolted through Orton Waterville with Prince Charles clinging desperately to its neck. What, if I may make so bold, is your problem?'

'You'd laugh if I told you.'

'I could use a good laugh this morning, old boy.'

'Where is Lord Wentworth's yacht moored?'

'It's usually at Cowes, of course. But at the present moment it's . . .'

'. . . in the Medway at Chatham.'

'That's right. How did you know?'

'A Bishop told me, *old boy*.'

'Then it must be true, mustn't it?'

I put the phone down. I'd had an idea. I picked it up again and got Dr Gervis. He's a G.P., a part-time police surgeon, and he didn't mind helping me out sometimes unofficially.

'What do you want, Bill?' he asked.

'You dabble a bit in psychiatry, don't you?'

'If we're being strictly accurate I'm interested in medical psychology, what you might call psychological motivation. I like to try to find out why people do some of the silly things they do. Especially criminals.'

'Could you talk to a man for me? Tell me if he's nuts?'

'For that you need a psychiatrist.'

'*Would* you talk to him for me? Tell me what you think.'

'I suspect from the tone of your voice that this is on the Q.T. again. Can you bring him in?'

'No, it'll have to be here. Interview room one.'

'That's better than the cells. It would have to be immediately. I have a surgery at one.'

'That suits me.'

'Can you brief me.'

'A man downstairs says he's kidnapped Prince Charles and that if he doesn't get a million pounds within eight hours – well, it's six and a half hours now – Prince Charles will die.'

'Did he say he'll *kill* Prince Charles. Specifically? That would make a difference.'

'No, he specifically said Prince Charles would die.'

'Obviously you don't believe him. There is no question he might be telling the truth? You've checked everything?'

'I've done *some* checking. I'm going to do a bit more.'

'I thought the Royals belonged to chief inspector and above.'

'They do.'

'So this really *is* on the Q.T. What do you want?'

'I want to know how to get rid of this man without doing him any harm. I can't explain why but I feel sorry for him. I suspect he's had a bad time. He was a prisoner in Korea.'

'That makes it easier. I'll be right around.'

Telephone again. Detectives' room again. 'Harry Ritchie there?' He came to the phone. Harry looks like one of those men who go round collecting on an insurance book. Not like a copper. 'Harry,' I said, 'how are you getting on with that jewellers' job?'

'Just about finished, Inspector. We're circulating a list of all the stuff. I was coming to see you to ask if I can walk about a bit. I think it was a planned job and somebody should have seen something.'

'Good idea. While you're out could you slot something in for me? No need to make a fuss. Sort of private.'

'You mean don't tell the chief?'

'You're too sharp, Harry. A man called James Bishop lives in Arlington Villas. Could you ask a few questions about him?'

'Right,' he said in his dry voice. I knew he'd come back with James Bishop's life story. He was that kind of copper. It would be all there down to the size of James Bishop's shoes. And nobody would ever remember they'd been questioned. Anonymity is a wonderful quality for a detective, the ability to stay in the background, see and not be seen, hear and not be heard. Harry had that.

I was restless, couldn't sit down. I went downstairs to the desk, told Sergeant Jones that Dr Gervis would be coming to interview room one and I didn't want it logged.

He nodded wisely. 'Best thing that could have happened,' he said. 'We had to hurt him a bit to get him out last time, poor devil.'

I carried on downstairs, signed the book and went into the cells. A drunk from the previous night was in the first cell, still lying in the vomit he'd have to clean up himself before he was taken to magistrates' court, which today wasn't until one o'clock. The cell in which the man had hanged himself was painted green and white with a brown stripe at eye-level. What a place to die! What a place to kill yourself! Further along was Cockney Alf. One of our regulars. We'd be charging him this afternoon for pick-pocketing. It would be the sixth time.

'Do me a favour, Alf, will you?' I said. 'Go and work some other patch.'

'I like it here,' he said in a cheerful nasal voice. 'You run a good nick. No kidding, Inspector, you make the best tea this side of the river, and your sausage and mash! A treat that is. But do us a favour, will you? Tell 'em to get in some HP Sauce.'

'You cheeky bugger,' I said, my good humour partly restored. Alf's an honest criminal and in his own quiet way makes a good living at it. Looking at him now in his smart suit, handmade shoes, sea island cotton shirt, he could have been James Bond. No wonder he worked our patch, where wallets really had something in them. He was a good dip but what I liked about him was that he never resorted to violence, never gave us an argument. When we caught him he always admitted it, usually came up with a list of offences to be 'taken into consideration', trying to be helpful. Cheeky bugger once said to me, 'Anything in my line you'd like me to confess to, take it off your book, do you a favour? As long as it's in my line.'

'Anything else you'd like while I'm ordering?' I said. 'A few potted shrimps, some smoked salmon?'

'Now who's being cheeky,' he said.

I told him what I'd come down for. 'You're being charged this afternoon. You've seen the papers?' I might have said we'll be signing a contract.

'Yes, I've seen them; they're all in order. You could do me a favour,' he said. 'Among my stuff there's a Patek Phillipe watch. It's not bent; there's a receipt with it. Stick it in your drawer and I'll pick it up when I get out.'

'I'll need a piece of paper from you. I don't want them thinking I've nicked it.'

'I'll give you that when they charge me,' he said, 'and thank you very much. You can wear it if you want to, give yourself a bit of class.'

I went back upstairs.

As I passed the desk Sergeant Jones nodded. 'He's in there,' he said. I knew he meant Dr Gervis and walked slowly up to my office.

I felt refreshed after seeing Alf. He'd helped me put things back in perspective. I get too involved sometimes. Bishop wasn't my affair. He belonged to the social workers, the people who understand his sort of mind. My speciality is the criminal mind. Men like Alf I can understand. Crime, detection, sentencing. The what and the how, the when and where, and primarily the who. Leave the why to the social workers, the head-shrinkers, the moralists. The only reason I ever wanted to know *why* was to help the criminal side of my investigation. Like that fellow Benton I was convinced had hit his wife with a hammer. If I could find a motive, if he had a bird on the side or hoped to collect on an insurance policy, I'd have information I could use to get a confession. Let's face it, I didn't care *why* he'd killed his wife. Man and woman live in faith and trust and understanding, forgiving faults, tolerating difficulties, content to spend their lives together. Sometimes it doesn't work out like that; the tolerance runs out, the little faults become big faults, the temporary minor irritations become monstrous and unforgivable errors, and the liquid of love turns violent and turbulent and someone strikes out. Often the blow is merely a way of expressing anger or frustration and once it's been delivered the anger is gone. Sometimes the blow has a more final purpose, the ending of a situation that has become utterly intolerable. For one person to end the life of another person is against the Law. And that's when I become involved.

But if what I said was true, why was I so concerned about Bishop? Why had I asked the doctor to come on the Q.T., used the chief inspector's number to speak to the Palace? If what I said was true the Law had nothing to do with James Bishop, and I should either throw him out or let them charge him with the only crime I suspected him of, Obstructing the Police in the Execution of their Duty.

I went out of the office and along the corridor to Superintendent Bowkes's room. He had a carpet on the floor. Adams had always wanted an office with a carpet and the rank of superintendent that went with it. He nearly made it once. Now the poor sod would be lucky if his wife remembered his name in three years' time.

'I've been thinking about the Benton job,' I said to Superintendent Bowkes. He sat back and shot his cuffs at me. His pink round face shone across the desk and he smelled of after-shave lotion.

'I wondered when you'd get around to that,' he said, unable to resist being pompous.

'I don't think it was an accidental death.'

'It isn't yet! It's a Death by Causes Unknown. It won't be an accidental death until the coroner says so; he can't say anything until you return that forensic report you're sitting on.'

Sitting on! Dammit, I hadn't had it half a day yet.

'It all depends where she was looking when the hammer hit her,' I said. 'There's no way we can get any corroborating evidence. In the Coroner's Court he's going to say she was looking at the floor. But I've got a hunch. . . .'

I could have bitten out my tongue. Me and my hunches. We were both famous. He lifted his hand. The cuticle of his nails gleamed as if he polished them. 'Spare me your *hunches*, Inspector. Even if I were foolish enough to believe them what good would they do? Can you imagine what the defending counsel will say in court if all we can come up with is one of Inspector Armstrong's well known hunches?'

'I know he killed his missis! The bastard's going to get away with it and I don't like that.'

'The Law says – beyond all shadow of a doubt. Can you truthfully say you have no doubt, no shadow of a doubt that he killed his wife? The chief superintendent wants to see all the papers today. They are pressing him to initiate the Coroner's Court. We can't flannel the chief superintendent with one of your hunches, I'm afraid.'

'Let them hold the Coroner's Court. It can always be Cause or Causes Unknown. That needn't close the investigation.'

I could see he didn't like it. Superintendent Bowkes has a fetish for tidiness. He doesn't like leaving cases open. Of course, it wasn't up to him to decide if Benton had murdered his wife. But if the coroner came out with a verdict of Accidental Death that would close the case so far as the superintendent was concerned. He likes nothing better than a closed case. It would be very hard for me to deploy my own and detective time to further investigation of a case that was officially closed. But hell, I didn't want Benton to get away with murdering his wife. All that crap about the perfect crime – and when you think of it this simple one had all the makings. Benton swings a hammer, cracks her skull, sets up the ladder, says the hammer fell. How could we prove otherwise. I had a sudden thought.

'When are you going to put in the papers, Superintendent?'

'They'll go in my Out-tray as soon as I've read them. My Out-tray is cleared at five o'clock.'

I got up to go.

'How are you getting on with the Murphy job?' he asked, still offering me that pink Palmolive smile. Crafty sod! Murphy was an Irish girl accused of complicity in a bomb job. So far we had over a hundred statements to go through, to sift and collate. It would leave me no time to worry about Benton. Or about Bishop, come to think of it.

'The papers are coming up this afternoon. I shall get started on them right away.'

'Good man. I wouldn't want any of your hunches to get in the way of real detective work.'

The warning was clear, the priorities clearly laid out. Murphy first; then you can mess about. Unless another crime comes along, and that wasn't unlikely at an average of two per day per officer. No wonder a half of them are never solved, never even come out of the folders.

I went back to my room. Telephoned to the detectives' room. 'Is Sergeant Williams there?'

There was a hollow laugh. 'He'll be here for ever, buried under a mountain of papers. . . .'

'The Murphy job?'

'What else? That girl had more witnesses than Lady Godiva. . . .'

The detective must have waved to Sergeant Williams, who took the telephone from him. 'Williams here,' he said in his lugubrious voice. He sounded like Paul Robeson singing tote that bar, lift that bale.

'Those Murphy papers. . . .'

'Don't, Inspector. I dream about them at nights. But at last there's a light at the end of the tunnel. You'll have them on your desk by half past one. . . .'

'So soon . . .?'

'That's a change of tune. You've been nagging me about them for four days. . . .'

'I know. But I've been a bit hasty. I hadn't realized quite how much work was involved. Why don't you give yourself a bit of a break? Bring them up, shall we say, tomorrow. . . .'

'Blimey, wonders will never cease. . . . I wouldn't mind resting my eyes for an hour or two. . . .'

'Good, let's say two o'clock tomorrow. Needn't say anything to Superintendent Bowkes about it. By the way, you were on that Benton job. Where are the photographs?'

'Right here. We're making up the package for the chief super. Going to Coroner's Court day after tomorrow, isn't it?'

'I wouldn't mind having another look at those pictures. Could you send them up?'

'Certainly – but she's no oil painting.'

'None of them are when they're dead.'

There was a knock at my door. 'Come in,' I shouted.

It was Dr Gervis. 'I've had a chat,' he said. 'Curious case. Wouldn't mind spending some time with him later.'

'What can you tell me?'

'Brief history. He was taken prisoner in the Korean war, captured, put in one of those holes for two years. You know about the holes?'

I shuddered. I'd heard stories, seen pictures. They dug holes in the ground, not wide enough for a man to lie down. Lined them with bamboo, put the man in there and left him. Some were there for as long as two years. Occasionally they throw food in, sometimes water; sometimes, just for fun, the guards would piss in it, even take a crap. Occasionally the men in the holes would be brought out, beaten and thrown back in again. Life can be a a terrible hell and still we go on doing it.

'The hole had a surprising effect on Bishop,' Dr Gervis said. 'Oddly enough it gave him the will to live. When he was finally released he came back and was demobilized. He tried various jobs but couldn't stick them for long. He always walked away so he could never get unemployment benefits. He's never committed a crime, so the authorities have never had him under care or supervision. He has no dependants, so he doesn't qualify for supplementary assistance benefits. He's just a piece of flotsam, drifting about as best he can, making a living as best he can. One of the tragedies of our modern civilization. He doesn't come into any category. He's not disabled in the physical sense of the word, he's not medically sick. He's just incapable of conforming to the routine of everyday life.'

'Did you find any criminal tendencies in him?'

'It's impossible to say on such a short acquaintance, but there were no overt signs. Understand, he doesn't rebel against men in authority, he's just afraid of them. They are his devil, if you like. His Prince of Darkness.'

I could remember Bishop crouched back against that wall, see again the terrible fear in his eyes. 'So what can we do about him . . .?'

'You'd better do something quite soon,' the doctor said. 'This story about Prince Charles. . . . I have the feeling – mind you, at the moment it's only a feeling and I've nothing solid on which to base it – that he could be telling the truth.'

I know Dr Gervis well. He isn't the man to say that kind of thing lightly. I understood there hadn't been time for a full examination and hadn't expected anything positive to come out of it. Frankly, I thought the doctor would say that Bishop was round the bend, though he'd put it in medical terms.

'I get the feeling,' the doctor said, 'that Bishop has come to the end of a long road. For the first time since he came out of that hole, he's made a decision about his own future. I think he's found the strength, at long last, to supplement that decision with action. I wasn't able to find anything in what he said that was irrational, that was medically identifiable as paranoia. He was completely logical. And free from malice. He knows the system can't bend to accommodate him, but thinks the people in it could be more flexible.'

'Can you give me an example . . .?'

'Yes, I can, a very clear one. The clerk Bishop sees at the Department of Employment is called Jackson. Jackson keeps cropping up in Bishop's conversation. Jackson, if you like, has become a symbol of "the System" to Bishop. Often a patient uses a real person as a symbol. If you like to think of it this way, it's a question of putting all your hatred, all your frustrations, on to the shoulders of one identifiable person who becomes "the enemy". Someone has said that we all need someone to love, and someone to hate. Jackson has become that "someone to hate". Ordinarily, this would be all right if there was the counterbalance of "someone to love". But Bishop has no such person, no such leavening force.'

'But you said there's no evidence of paranoia . . .?'

Dr Gervis smiled. 'Paranoia and hatred aren't the same thing,' he said. 'We all have hatred in us, fortunately. Hatred is a safety valve, a normal expression of extreme dislike. Paranoia is a conviction of persecution, a feeling that the other person is trying, in malevolent ways, to harm or damage us. Bishop has none of that. That's why I think that, strange, even impossible as it may seem, he could be telling his version of the truth about Prince Charles.'

CHAPTER THREE

One fifth of November, when I was a constable, I was walking a beat in Portland Place. Fireworks were exploding everywhere in the back streets, a harmless celebration of the death of a traitor few people remembered. Round the back of Portland Place, in a short mews where once they kept carriages, somebody had lighted a small bonfire. A few egg crates, fruit boxes, a couple of worm-eaten bentwood chairs. Half a dozen kids squatted round the fire; one of them had a potato on a long metal rod. He'd stuck the potato into the embers and would have roasted it if he hadn't kept pulling it out to look at it. 'Leave it in there,' I said, and walked away to continue my beat, grateful for the two minutes' heat on the cold November night.

A man detached himself from a group of parents standing by a bench on which they were lighting fireworks, Golden Rain, Red Sunburst, and Fiery Rocket – I love the names – while they held the too inquisitive kids back and handed out flaming Sparklers. The man was bundled up in a duffel coat and I could see little of his face under the hood. When he spoke, his voice was muffled by the wool and seemed to come from deep inside him.

'It's got nothing to do with me, Constable. . . .'

That's a standard opening which we tend to ignore. In those days I was inexperienced and therefore became instantly suspicious.

'It's got nothing to do with me, Constable, but there's been a girl standing on that balcony all the time we've had the fire going. She just stands there, and doesn't move. It puts a shiver down me, just watching her. . . .'

I looked up to where he pointed. The south side of the mews was a tall building ten storeys high. High windows on each floor; some with subdued lights behind them. Some black, like eye-sockets. In a couple of the windows the curtains were drawn and I could see faces pressed to the windows, children who'd been allowed to stay up late, but not to come out into the cold air. Possibly their parents thought them too special to mix with the common folk.

At the top of the building was a low decorative iron rail and behind it a mansard roof sloping back. There were windows in the roof – rooms possibly once used for servants, now in demand as studios. A girl had climbed out of one of the windows and was standing braced against the roof, holding one of the buttresses. The rail was only about twelve inches high. It didn't look a safe place to be.

'How long has she been there?'

'The fire's been going for the best part of an hour.'

I went into the back door of the building that opened on to the mews. A rickety old lift rattled me slowly to the ninth floor. I got out, glad to walk the other floor. At the top was a short corridor, with four doors leading off it. The doors were old and had been varnished without scraping; the channels in the old varnish ran like rivers. One door was wide open. It seemed to be about the place I had seen the girl. I tapped on it. There was no reply. A short passage extended beyond the door, with two more doors leading off it to the left. Almost blocking the end of the corridor was a large cupboard painted in green and yellow. At that point, the corridor became the main living room, or so it seemed. I saw the arm of a sofa, covered in leather cloth, with the edges of it scuffed and holed. A piece of the yellow stuffing stuck out, as if someone had pulled nervously at it.

There was no reply to my knock.

I took off my hat, cradled it in my arm, and walked into the flat. When I reached the yellow and green cupboard, I tapped gently on the side of it and coughed before looking round the corner. A policeman, we'd been told over and over again, has no automatic right of entry. I tapped again. Still no reply, so I poked my head round the side of the cupboard and looked into the room. It was empty, and ice-cold. There was an elaborate fireplace of brown speckled marble with a black painted iron fire basket. No fire had been lit there in a long time. An electric convector heater stood at the side of the fireplace but didn't appear to be switched on. The room was very tidy. Table in the centre with books on it. No sign of food. Far side of the room a kitchenette, to judge from the cups hanging on hooks on a shelf.

The room had three windows. The one on the left was open. I could see the girl standing in the narrow rain gully. To her left was the sloping buttress that gave her privacy from the next flat, as well as supporting the mansard wall. She was looking down.

'Hello!' I called, making my voice loud enough for her to hear, not loud enough to startle her.

She turned and looked back into the room. Twenty-five, twenty-six? Wearing a pullover and skirt. Hair long and nicely brushed, though blown a bit by the wind. It was cold in the flat. It would be colder where she was. Her face was lighted from below in a rainbow of flaring lights which doubtless came from the fireworks. Occasionally, it would be dark. I could hear a thin rumble of voices from below in the mews, but not distinguish any words. I walked slowly across the room towards the window, and put my helmet on the table. She'd turned back, indifferent to my being there. I don't think she'd registered my presence at all. Her face was drawn and white. She didn't look ill or anything, just drawn. When I got to the window I could see that what I had feared was true; she was leaning out.

I couldn't think what to say at first. I stood there, at a loss for words, not knowing what to do. I was young then, and had never seen a suicide. If that's what she was. I'd look a fool if she was only admiring the fireworks, wouldn't I, and in those days I cared about not looking a fool.

'Are you the owner of this flat?' I asked, trying to keep my voice on a monotone. Routine inquiry, I hoped the tone would imply.

She nodded.

'Could I have a word with you . . .?'

I hoped she'd think it was something to do with the rent or the rates; or had she seen anything suspicious, appealing to her sense of good citizenship to help the Law. In all its Majesty. I didn't feel very majestic.

'Go away,' she said. Her voice was a whisper in the dark night. The fireworks had gone out, all was darkness. Now I could distinguish the boisterous shouts of the children below.

'Go away,' she said.

It wasn't a defiant command; it sounded more like an entreaty, and that gave me courage. I started to climb through the window. She was four feet away from me. Once I was half out, I could grab her. She moved to the very edge of the rain gutter.

'Go away,' she said again.

I think she thought I could do that, just turn my back on her and walk away down the street whistling.

'Now come along, Miss,' I said, aware of my own inadequacy, feeling like someone who comes in half way through a film and doesn't know the story, is confused by the plot and the characters. She made a small gesture, pointing downwards.

'I wanted it,' she said, 'I wanted to have it. . . .'

I was trying to inch my way forward, awkwardly balanced in that window frame, half in, half out, seeing only the girl's skirt and her jumper in the darkness and the lighter blur of her face. My hand was holding the window frame. I'd have to change my balance so that I no longer needed its support, so that I could lunge outwards and catch hold of her skirt, drag her back inside. I braced my knee against the lower ledge.

'Wanted what, Miss?' I asked, hoping to keep her talking so that she wouldn't notice my movements.

But then she jumped.

I lunged and grabbed but my hand came nowhere near her. As she went I shouted, and the sound of my voice seemed to hang on the black night like a cloak. Long before she hit the ground I heard the screams start, short and staccato, like a rook condemned.

The forensic boys put the story together.

She'd had an abortion. I'd seen a piece of paper on the table, and made a mental note of Mrs Sybil Karos, 14 Dalton Grove, Shepherd's Bush. Dalton Grove is at the sleazy end of Shepherd's Bush; it seemed an unlikely address for a girl like this to keep.

On my next day off I went to see Mrs Karos. She turned out to be a Cypriot crone as dirty as she was avaricious, a spider at the centre of a filthy web of illegal operations. One by one I traced some of her victims and the network that had recommended them. When I had the package ready I took it to my sergeant and he handed it to the Detective Division. That was not only how I started as a detective but how I acquired a reputation for sticking my nose in where it wasn't wanted. The Detective Division had written off the death of that girl, had made no attempt to follow up that Shepherd's Bush address. I started my life as a detective already on the wrong foot.

Dr Gervis had to return to his practice to get ready for his one o'clock surgery. I glanced at the clock: it was 12.15. Now we had only five hours and forty-five minutes to Bishop's eight-hour deadline.

I went up to the chief inspector's office. The chief inspector likes to eat at the same time and in the same place every day. They say he goes through the menu at Manolo's dish by dish then starts back at the beginning again. It's a standing Station joke that one day we'll get Manolo to put snails on the list and frogs' legs right after the steamed cod. Some of the lads would bet quite heavily that the chief wouldn't notice.

He was standing up and reaching for his hat when I got there. It's a green felt pork-pie with a brown leather strap round it. Nobody can remember a time he didn't wear it winter or summer. It goes well with his sports jacket and grey flannel bags, which somehow are always impeccably creased. He didn't move from the hat rack when I went into his office.

'Are you coming for a bite of dinner?' he asked.

'And risk food poisoning?'

'Never harmed *me*.'

'You've developed an immunity to Manolo's food over the years.' I sat down in the chair in front of the desk.

He sighed, put his hat back on the rack and sat in his own chair behind the desk. 'You have that look on your face,' he said, 'that tells me the cod is going to be off when I get to Manolo's.'

'I thought this was the spaghetti day?'

'Cheeky bugger. What's on your mind?'

'Bishop.'

'You must be as crazy as he is. Little old lady stopped me on the steps yesterday as I was coming in, told me she was the Tzarina of Russia and asked me to arrange her trip back to

Moscow. I said "if you've got the money I'll send somebody round to Thomas Cook's." She told me to see the Royal Chamberlain. She said, "You are Ivan Ivanovich, aren't you?" I said, "No, I'm Pavlov Pavlovich." She said, "Sorry" and went away! I'm still not Ivan Ivanovich you know; I'm Chief Inspector Roberts and you're Detective Inspector Armstrong, not Sir Galahad, and this is a police station, not a home for the mentally incurable.'

'Item one: Bishop knows that Prince Charles is wearing a grey lounge suit today. . . .'

'A grey lounge suit is a uniform to the aristocracy. If Prince Charles were opening the Fishmongers' Hall in Ipswich he'd be wearing a dark *blue* lounge suit. Come off it, Bill!'

'All right then, item two: he knows that Lord Wentworth's yacht is moored in the Medway off Chatham though normally it's moored at Cowes.'

'So he's picked up a copy of *Yachting World* in the library, or he reads Jennifer. "Guess who I saw mincing up the muddy Medway in his yukki yacht . . . none other than wonderful Willi Wentworth with charming Charlie on board . . ."'

'Dr Gervis says he's a loner, that he doesn't trust anybody or anything. He thinks he's telling the truth.'

Chief Inspector Roberts reared up in his chair as if he'd been stung in the arse by a hot bee.

'Who the hell told you to call in Dr Gervis? I told you to get rid of that bugger, to throw him out. You told me you *had* thrown him out.'

His eyes were bulbous and staring, and anger spit formed on his lips. I'd seen him that way before. I knew I would see him that way again. He picked up the telephone. 'Get me the Palace,' he said. He held the telephone in his hand but looked at me, his eyes spitting sparks. With his free hand he drummed on the table top, obviously holding back a flood of words. When the Palace came on the line he said his number. With his free hand he'd depressed the talk-back button that activated the small speaker on his desk. He put the phone on the cradle. Now he was free to drum on the desk with both hands. He gave a fair imitation of Gene Krupa. 'Terribly sorry to bother you again,' he said, 'but can you tell me once and for all where

Prince Charles is at this precise moment?'

The voice came over the loudspeaker clipped, precise, but oh so bored. 'He's taken a day off! He's sailing on Lord Wentworth's yacht. We can't tell you precisely because, strange though it may seem, we don't keep a radar fix on every single member of the Royal Family.'

'You've got a man on the boat, of course.'

'Every moment of his life we keep a man close to Prince Charles. It's one of the burdens the Royal Family has to bear, like Divisions ringing up all the time asking where they are!'

I was grateful to him for speaking the way he did. It gave the inspector another target for his anger.

'Don't get shirty with me,' the chief inspector said, 'you Palace ponce. If some of you chaps would move out of that cloistered cocoon and do some real police work from time to time . . .'

'Superintendent James here. To whom am I speaking?' the voice said.

I groaned inwardly. Superintendent James had been a legend at Scotland Yard. He was the one who'd broken the Mussoli gang. And that was after they'd snapped his leg in three places.

'Chief Inspector Roberts, Sir. I apologize. I'm afraid I let my tongue run away with me.' He glared at me. 'But I was provoked.'

A chuckle came over the loudspeaker. 'I know those days, Chief Inspector. Don't give it another thought. You're quite right of course; it is too damned easy to sit here and criticize. Now what's your problem?'

The chief inspector told him calmly and factually. When the time came he let me report at first hand what the doctor had said. The superintendent listened to it all.

'It's the sort of thing we get all the time,' he said, 'but we won't discount it because of that. I'll initiate a few inquiries and get back to you. Is that okay?'

'That's fine, Sir,' the chief inspector said, 'and once again I'm sorry about the crack.'

'Don't give that another thought,' the superintendent replied and we heard the click as he hung up.

The chief inspector ran his hand across his face as if trying to flatten its features. 'I don't know what to do with you,' he said. 'You're like a bulldog. Every time you get your teeth into something it's impossible to prise you off. For once will you leave this to the right people? Bishop's a nut, believe me. You saw the way he backed against that wall. You saw the state his hands are in. I sympathize with him. The poor bugger's obviously been through the mangle; but we just don't have the time or the men to mess about with every screwball who walks through that front door. I'm going for my dinner and if you say a single word to stop me I'll clap you in the bloody cells along with that drunk.'

He came round the side of his desk, and put his hand on my shoulder. 'Leave it alone, Bill,' he said. Then he put the porkpie hat on his head and went out.

I went back down towards my office. I suddenly remembered Bishop was still in the interview room and carried on down there.

'Come on,' I said, 'I'll buy you a dinner. A place round the back does a nice steak and kidney.'

'Only five and a half hours left,' he said, 'but if you want to waste the time eating steak and kidney, I don't mind.'

CHAPTER FOUR

Tony runs a good clean café and his steak and kidney contains real kidney and a crisp crust. The twelve o'clock rush had died down and only two tables were occupied. When he saw us come in, Tony wiped his cloth over the table in the alcove, sensing I'd welcome a bit of privacy.

'The soup's good today, Governor,' he said, looking at Bishop. I guess he could sense Bishop could use some nourishment. I nodded. *'Due minestrone!'* he called out.

I never knew why he flashed his Italian about. He was born in Stepney, and his wife who did the cooking came from Belfast.

We sat down. Bishop appeared listless and indifferent to his surroundings. The smell of food and cooking hung thick in the air, pleasant, stimulating, not like the majority of oily so-called restaurants in the neighbourhood, where they bought supplies pre-adulterated by wholesalers and waved glossy menus full of hyperbole. Tony never had a menu, only good solid cooking. I breathed in a lungful—it contained more calories than a slice of bread.

'God, I'm hungry,' I said. 'What would you like to drink?' Tony's café isn't licensed but he had a neat arrangement for friends. I was lucky enough to count myself one of them. Steak and kidney pie cost forty pence; steak and kidney pie with sauce cost a little more, but the sauce had a froth on it and you drank it out of a glass.

'I don't drink,' Bishop said. 'I've got out of the habit. With everything you've got to do when we get back you ought to think about keeping a clear head.'

'What are you then, a Quaker . . . ?'

He shook his head. 'There's nothing abnormal about me and the sooner you accept that the better.'

'You do yourself an injustice,' I said. 'For any man to have the nerve to come into a police station with a story like you're trying to tell me is abnormal. Either it's abnormally brave, or abnormally stupid. Look, if all you wanted to do was have yourself arrested, to find a comfortable billet in gaol for a week or two, why not throw a brick through a jeweller's shop window . . . ?'

'Like the man in the O. Henry story . . . ?'

I nodded. The temptation was strong to make this a normal conversation, to go on to say, yes, and did you see Charles Laughton in the film, and so on. . . . But dammit, this wasn't the time for that sort of chatter. He'd given us a deadline for a death; who was going to be killed didn't matter since the police force works on the premise that *all* human life is sacred, just like the medical profession.

'Did you see Charles Laughton in the film?' he said, and I laughed. Don't tell me the bugger was also a mind reader. . . .

'No, I didn't,' I said, lying to keep him off the subject.

'In the days when it was the Odeon, you could get into that one along Arlington Street via the gents' lavatory,' he said. 'The lock didn't work. I spent many an hour in there, watching the films . . .'

'Instead of working . . . ?'

He nodded.

'Is that where you concocted this scheme to con us out of a million pounds? You can't believe all you see in the films.'

'They'd have written the plot in a more dramatic way. You have to admit, I haven't involved you in a drama. Letters cut out of the newspapers, stuck on to a piece of Woolworth's paper. Telephone calls in a masked voice. All that stuff.'

'I wish you had. That's not my department.'

'You're not enjoying this much, are you, Inspector?'

'No, frankly, I'm not. I like real crime. Real villains. I like chasing people who have criminal minds. So far, I don't think you're a villain.' To explain what I meant, I told him about the Benton case, all about it. He seemed interested. '*That's* a man with a criminal mind,' I said. 'He thinks he can commit a crime like that and get away with it. I see it as a game of chess, and I'm determined to beat him. But *you*, you don't have that kind of mind. I think you came in to the station spontaneously. I think you got carried away. Had this crazy dream you could get a million pounds out of us. But you can't, you know, and the sooner you accept that, the better.'

'The immovable object, eh, Inspector?'

'And you think of yourself as the irresistible force.' I was getting narked. I could see that none of my attempts to help him were having any effect. When he smiled, he concealed an inner conviction; when he agreed with something I said, it was as if *he* were humouring *me*, as if I were the one with the crazy demands.

'Somehow you've got to realize,' I said, 'that we're all in the same boat. We all have to live with officialdom. None of us likes it, but we think it preferable to the anarchy of everybody going his own way. Somehow, you've got to learn to fit into the system. You keep telling yourself you're different, because of what has happened to you in your life. But you're not in a position to be different. You've got to learn to fit in with the patterns of *real* life, not some invented Nirvana. You've got to learn that you can only get on in life by being *normal*, by behaving *normally*.'

'I keep telling you, Inspector. There's nothing abnormal about me. . . .'

I banged my hand on the table. 'That's where you're wrong,' I said. 'There *is* something abnormal about you. This obsession with Prince Charles and this kidnapping, you won't leave it alone, will you? You keep rabbiting on about it. Look Jim, or James if you prefer it, I'm not going to give you a million pounds, because you haven't kidnapped Prince Charles. All right, you've done what you set out to do, you've given the police something to think about. You've had your moment of glory. If it's any satisfaction you've made the police chase about. Right now they're checking that Prince Charles is where you know he is. Knock it off, will you, have your dinner and let's call it a day!'

His eyes had a faraway look. 'I've just been thinking while you were talking of the way I would go about an investigation like this if I were a policeman. . . .'

He hadn't even been listening to me. How could I get through to him? How could I stop him sliding down this path that would inevitably mean further degradation? I didn't want to do that to him. I could see the poor man had suffered all his life; I didn't want to add to it. But there wasn't time, there just wasn't time.

He ate every mouthful of the minestrone. I saw that Tony had given him a double portion, had obviously dredged extra vegetables out of the pot for him. When the steak and kidney pie came that was a double portion too. Tony had eyes in his head and we could both see clearly that Bishop hadn't been feeding himself properly. When I paid the bill I took out an extra five pound note. I give myself pocket money every week out of the housekeeping. I think a man needs that to keep his self-respect. For the same reason I always insist Sarah keeps a pound or two in her purse for her own small purchases. I stuck the five pound note in the top pocket of Bishop's coat.

'Take it,' I said, 'I can always get it back on expenses.'

That was a lie but he wasn't to know. Introduce him to Nancy, that's what I'd do. Kill two birds with one stone. It'd get Nancy off my back, relieve Sarah's suspicions. Bishop and Nancy would get on together and looking after that fourteen-year-old boy would give Bishop an interest outside himself. I scribbled Nancy's address on a piece of paper.

'Use some of that money,' I said, 'to take a taxi to this address.'

I knew I'd have time to get on the telephone to brief Nancy to expect him. I could visualize his face, padded out with some of Nancy's food. A few lights put back into those dull and listless eyes. Whatever else she might be, Nancy was jolly and she'd kid him along a bit. She'd have him in bed with her within a week and that could bring back his self-respect.

We left the café together; I looked for a taxi for him, relieved to have found the solution.

'I'm coming back to the station with you,' he said. 'You can take the five pounds out of my million.'

I lost my temper. 'Piss off,' I shouted. Passers-by turned to stare but I didn't care.

I turned and walked rapidly back to the station, head down, barging through groups of people and not caring, my mind a fire of blazing bewildered anger fuelled by the terrible black sense of my own inadequacy. 'I bought him lunch,' I kept saying to myself, 'why can't he leave me alone?' As if the minestrone and the steak and kidney pie had absolved me of all other responsibilities. I was talking to myself. 'I've got things to do. Important things. I'm a copper, not a wet-nurse!'

When I walked into the station and across the entrance lobby, everybody was looking. But not at me; at the figure of James Bishop, following a neat three strides behind me, like a shadow.

I led the way into interview room one. He followed me and sat down. 'That was a good lunch,' he said. 'Thank you very much.'

'Listen to me very carefully. A superintendent is checking the whereabouts of Prince Charles. I'm going to ring him. That's the last thing I'm going to do for you. If you don't go after I've spoken to him, I shall tell them to throw you out again, and if you try to come back into the front door they'll put you in the cells downstairs. You'll be charged with whatever the Legal Department thinks is appropriate. I'll make damned certain you never see me and I never see you again, except in court. You need help, James, I'm quite aware of that. But I'm not the person to give it to you.'

I wrote down Dr Gervis's name and address. 'Go and see that doctor,' I said, 'and he'll look after you. He won't cost you anything. He's the man to help you, not me. Go and see that woman whose name and address I gave you in the café. She'll give you somewhere decent to live, a few jobs around the house to take your mind off your own troubles. She's a good, kind, woman, and she could use the help you can give her, so it won't be charity.' I put my hand on his arm, felt him flinch involuntarily at the first contact. 'I'm sorry, James, truly I'm sorry I can't help you any more. When you're settled in with that lady, I'll come and see you at the house when I'm off-duty and there's a bit more time for a chat. Do you play chess? Perhaps we could have a game of chess together....'

'You're a warm and generous man,' he said, acknowledging for the first time that he had thoughts outside his Prince Charles fantasy. 'I can't imagine you letting another man die in four hours.'

Damn him. I glanced at the clock on the wall. Two o'clock. We had wasted half his 'eight hours'.

I picked up the telephone, got through to the chief inspector. 'Have you heard from Superintendent James, Chief?' I asked.

When he spoke his voice was quite mellow. The cod must have been 'on' at Manolo's, or maybe he'd had a second beer.

'Not yet,' he said, 'but even superintendents have to eat you know.'

'You mind if I give him a ring?'

'If it'll make you feel better and help towards getting your mind off Bishop and on to police work again.'

I rang Superintendent James at the Palace. When I'd identified myself, he said, 'I imagine you were the one provoking the chief inspector. Right?'

'I suppose I was, Superintendent. May I ask if you've spoken to the prince?'

'I heard about you and that caper at the Royal Hall.'

'That was a long time ago, Superintendent. Have you spoken to the prince?'

'Persistent chap, aren't you? No, I haven't spoken to him yet.'

My heart sank. 'Why not?'

'People usually address me as Superintendent, Inspector.'

'Sorry, Sir.'

'One thing you learn as you achieve senior rank, Inspector, is to take the balanced view. All cases are equally important. You're quite right to push but you mustn't go overboard, you know. I haven't spoken to Prince Charles because the coastguard station at Chatham can't get a reply from Lord Wentworth's yacht. The yacht sailed out this morning; right now it's probably somewhere off the mouth of the Thames; so far we haven't been able to pinpoint it, and we haven't been able to get a radio reply. Before your mind goes rushing away into some dark tragedy let me explain that there could be a hundred valid reasons why we can't raise them. Their radio might not be switched on, or it may be faulty. They may be in a skip distance area. Their batteries could be flat. We'll keep on trying and I'll give you a ring. And now may I respectfully suggest you put this matter to one side of your blotter and get on with the hundreds of other things I know an inspector must have to do.' He put the phone down.

He was quite right, of course. They pay superintendents to be right. But they pay inspectors to expose themselves to the chance of being wrong.

I turned back to Bishop. 'You must have known you were taking a chance when you walked in here,' I said, 'a chance we'd dump you in the cells and charge you.'

Bishop stood up, unbuttoned his jacket, unbuttoned his shirt beneath it and pulled it wide. He wasn't wearing an undervest. I winced as I looked at his body. His chest was a mess of scars that defied description.

'One thing you haven't realized,' he said, 'is that I'm past caring what anybody might do to me. You can't frighten me. For a start, I bet your cells are a lot warmer and more comfortable than the basement room I spend my life in at Arlington Villas. And you appear to eat a lot better than I've been used to.' He sat down again, not bothering to button up his shirt but drawing his coat around him to hide those terrible scars.

'What sort of a man are you?' I said.

'Now we're getting down to it. I can see that you no longer dismiss me as being insane. I'm just an ordinary man who's been caught up in a civilization that interprets the word ordinary in a very different way from me.'

'What's your job? What do you do for a living?'

'I've done everything at one time or another. My friend Mr Jackson' – he gave a hollow laugh. 'If you feel frustrated dealing with me you ought to see Mr Jackson's face every time I walk in.'

'I take it Mr Jackson is with the Department of Employment.'

'I never remember what they call it. I always think of it as the Labour Exchange.'

'I imagine you can't hold down a job. Probably have no skill, no trade.'

'That's where you're wrong. I've got all the skills, all the trades. You name it and Mr Jackson has tried me at it. I've worked a lathe, a milling machine, a horizontal boring machine. I've soldered parts of time clocks, I've swept up in a factory, pushed tree trunks through a circular saw, wrapped parcels, sold cloth from a market stall. Currently I'm pushing a mop for a Contract Cleaning Company. Well I was until yesterday, but I imagine they're busy firing me because I haven't turned up. That's the wrong thing to say. They won't fire me because otherwise they might get into an argument about redundancy. When Mr Jackson rings them up they'll tell him the truth, that I walked off the job.'

'And that means you won't get any unemployment pay.'

'That's right; since I'm a single man I don't qualify for Supplementary Benefits either. I don't think Mr Jackson will find me another job.'

'Why can't you stay on the job? Don't you like working?'

'I love it. I like being with other people. I like talking to other people.'

'According to the doctor you don't. You prefer being on your own.'

His face lost its look of composure. 'You know how it is; after a while people get on your nerves, talking all the time, asking you things: where do you come from, what do you do, how did you get your hands like that . . .?'

That would be it, of course. 'How did you get your hands like that?' The intrusive questions or – and this was probably worse – the obtrusive non-questions, people looking at those terrible hands, shuddering, turning their eyes away and making no comment at all except behind his back.

'Someone like me just doesn't fit in,' he said. 'I don't know if I can explain it to you. I'm like a man who has an incredible lust for alcohol knowing that the first drink will make him sick. Society doesn't have any room for a man like me. I tried to work, I tried to earn a living for myself so that I won't be a burden to anybody. I had a marvellous job once, switchboard operator, thirty lines. I went there in the morning and nobody saw me arrive except the doorman. I went into the switchboard room and sat there all day answering the telephone, plugging the lines in, pulling the lines out and at the end of the day I closed down the switchboard, said good night to the doorman, and went home. But, you know, even that twice a day contact used to bother me. I'd get so that I waited until the doorman turned his back then try to slip in and out without him seeing me. The final blow was one day; he came to the switchboard room at twelve o'clock, brought his sandwiches and his thermos of tea with him. "I'll just come and eat my snap with you," he said, "we old soldiers got to stick together" and then he went rambling on, told me how he'd been wounded at Arras and gassed on the Somme. I couldn't stand it. I had to get out of that switchboard room. It was four hours before I could bring myself to go back and by then they'd rung up the Labour Exchange and Jackson had sent a young girl to do it.'

'Now you think the world owes you a living, eh?' It was a cheap thing to say and he knew it.

'I don't care what the world owes me,' he said, 'but I mean to have one of two things. Either a million pounds or life imprisonment. The Bank of England can turn out a few more notes – nobody will ever miss them – or you can lock me up somewhere, feed me and clothe me and keep me warm until the day I die. I don't care.'

'All right,' I said. 'If that's the way you want it, I shall ring this bell twice and two constables will come in as they came in before. You know what will happen. This time if you walk back into the station they'll put you in a cell. I shall make a statement to the Legal Department and they will decide what to prosecute you for. When they throw you out it's your decision. I've given you the addresses of two people who can and will help you. If you walk back into this station no power on earth can prevent the Law taking its course.'

'You sound just like Mr Jackson,' he said.

The door opened, the chief inspector came in. 'Can I have a word, Bill?' he said and I followed him out to the corridor. 'I've been talking with Superintendent James,' he said. 'They can't raise Lord Wentworth's yacht. Normally they wouldn't bother but you seem to have impressed the Super. Somebody's coming from Scotland Yard to take the case over. Is that what you wanted?'

I was deeply relieved. Of course I would have liked to see the thing through myself but I knew that was impossible. Divisional Detective Inspectors don't handle cases which involve Royal Personages, especially not the Heir to the Throne. 'That's good,' I said.

'And now maybe you can get back to the Murphy case,' the chief said.

I nodded, making a mental note that I'd look at the Benton

case first. I went back upstairs; the long afternoon stretched ahead. Nominally I was on duty until six o'clock, but tonight I'd be glad to get home.

When I got to my office I dialled my home number. There was no reply. I let the phone ring for three or four minutes but no one picked it up. That was strange. Sarah would be home if Helen were in bed. I knew her too well to believe she'd slip out while Helen was lying there sick. I had a sudden thought. Perhaps the doctor had been and given her a prescription and she'd slipped out to the chemist's. But in that case why hadn't Helen picked up the phone? Perhaps she was more ill than Sarah had said. I put down the telephone quickly so as not to waken her.

Benton. The photographs were in a neat package. Shots of the body lying on the floor, blood around the head. General shot of the windows, the stepladder, the pelmet hanging at an angle. A downwards shot of the body on the carpet taken from the ladder top, the view that Benton would have seen after the hammer dropped. If he was telling the truth, if he'd been on top of the ladder. A shot of the carpet after the body and the ladder had been moved away. In colour. Blood spots, dust. A couple of woodshavings, the four indentations of the feet of the stepladder. In one of the indentations were several spots of blood. I flipped open my notebook, found the page where I'd recorded the interview with Benton. Some people are surprised to learn I do short-hand. I've trained myself, Pitman system. It comes naturally to me and I'm as quick as any secretary when I care to be. It was all there.

Q: And this is exactly how it was? You haven't moved anything? That ladder, for instance?

A: No, I haven't moved anything. I was standing up on that ladder and I dropped the hammer. God, I'll never forgive myself.

'*I haven't moved anything!*'

The phrase leapt off the page at me. If he hadn't moved anything how had her blood got under the foot of that ladder? The ladder had been put there when she was lying on the carpet. 'Right, you bugger, I'll get you,' I said to myself. I knew I would too. I'd hammer away at that one question –

How did that blood get under that ladder? – until I broke him. I had another thought. Trajectories. If the forensic boys were clever they might be able to reconstruct the moment at which the blood started to come out of her body. They might even be able to prove how she was standing at the moment the hammer hit her. We had a full set of pictures they could work from.

The telephone rang. It was Sarah. 'I've been trying to get you for the last three hours but every time I phoned either your line's been engaged or you've been out.'

'I only went around the corner for a spot of dinner,' I said. 'Why didn't you leave a message?'

'I didn't like to!'

'Why not?' Then I heard a bit of a sob in her voice. 'Oh Bill . . .'

'Nothing serious with Helen, is it?'

'Her appendix. It all blew up quickly. I've been worried out of my mind. It burst in the ambulance.'

'What burst?'

'Her appendix.' Now she was sobbing.

'Steady on love. Tell me what's happened. Last time I talked to you she had an upset stomach.'

'I know,' she wailed. 'That's what I thought it was. The doctor took one look at her when he came at eleven o'clock and got on the phone right away for an emergency ambulance. I've never seen him so worried. I didn't know an appendix could blow up so quickly. They had an ambulance here in five minutes. I tried to phone you. They rolled her in a blanket and practically ran out of the house with her. I only had time to grab my coat and my purse and we were off. It burst on the way. Oh Bill, it was awful. They pulled the ambulance into the car park of the *Red Lion*. I couldn't bring myself to look. Dr Williams had to operate right then and there. I had to give my permission. Then we raced off again.'

'But she's all right now?'

Her voice was a long time in coming. 'No, Bill.'

'What do you mean, no?'

'She's got . . . they called it peritonitis. She's in the Intensive Care Unit on the danger list.' Now she was crying and her words were chopped up with sobs. 'I've tried to ring you, Bill, over and over again. I couldn't leave a message, not to tell you our Helen was on the danger list, I mean it would have been such a terrible shock for you.'

'Where is she?'

'St Matthew's. They took her into the first place. They were racing against time. Oh, Bill.'

'Where are you phoning from?'

'From the lobby.'

'I'll be right there. Don't go away. And love, I'm sorry you couldn't get me on the phone. It's just one of those silly things. Don't worry, she'll be all right; they have marvellous drugs nowadays. I'll be right over. Stay where you are and don't worry.' I put down the phone and was halfway out of the office when it rang again.

'Chief Detective Superintendent Pope from Scotland Yard has arrived,' Sergeant Jones said. 'I've put him in interview room two.'

'I'm going out. Put him in one with Bishop.'

'He wants to see you first.'

'Tell him I've gone out.'

'I'm afraid I've already told him you're in the building.'

'I don't give a cat in bloody hell what you've already told him,' I shouted. 'My wife's just been on the phone and they've got my daughter in St Matthew's with peritonitis and I'm going to see her.' I chucked the phone on to the desk not even bothering to put it back on its cradle and raced out of my room and down the corridor. A constable had just come up the steps with a tray of papers and I sent them flying out of his hand as I raced past him.

'I'm sorry,' I shouted, 'I'm sorry', turned the corner and flew down the steps that led to the lobby. A huge figure blocked the stairs at the bottom on the left. I went to the right and the figure dodged to the right. I dodged to the left and the figure moved to the left.

'Move out of it,' I shouted.

A large hand came out like an iron rod, grabbed me by the chest and held me still. 'Detective Inspector Armstrong?' the large man asked. 'I'm Chief Detective Superintendent Pope.'

'Can't stop, Chief. Daughter's in St Matthew's. Peritonitis.'

'Steady on, old lad.' His hand didn't move from my chest.

'I can't stop. He's in one. Got to go. I'll be back soon. He's in one.'

'Inspector Armstrong!' he said. 'Stand . Still . And . Shut . Up!'

I did as he said, deflated, defeated. He looked at me.

'Until you compose yourself, man, you're in no condition to go anywhere. Certainly not behind the wheel of a motor car. Come in here and sit down.'

He led me into interview room two. There was no way I could refuse him. My head was spinning with the news Sarah had given me, a fragmented horror picture of a doctor operating on my Helen in the car park of a public house.

'I've just heard they've taken my daughter into St Matthew's Hospital. She had an appendix which burst and apparently now she has peritonitis.'

'That's bad!' he said.

'My wife's waiting for me in the lobby of the hospital. She's very worried.'

'She would be, poor soul.' He picked up the telephone. '47059, quickly!' he said. I've never got a phone call as quickly as that.

'Harry,' he said, 'send Linda round to St Matthew's Hospital right away. Inspector Armstrong's wife is in the lobby. His daughter is in the Intensive Care Unit. Ask Linda to tell Mrs Armstrong her husband is unavoidably detained but that he'll be along just as soon as possible. Make certain Mrs Armstrong has everything she needs. . . .'

'She needs *me*,' I shouted, 'not a policewoman! She needs her husband, the father of her daughter who, for all you care, could be dying right now.'

He put down the telephone, came back across the room.

'The last thing your wife needs at a moment like this is a half hysterical husband involved in a motor car accident. Until you relax, you're not going anywhere. Anyway, man, think logically. Your daughter is in the Intensive Care Unit, and that's damned bad for any father, but there's nothing you can do. A hundred to one they won't even let you see her; they'll be too busy saving her life to trot in and out with information. Calm down. Then go and see your wife. Take her out for a cup of tea. Be calm and helpful to her, not hysterical, going off half cock. Meanwhile, you can sit still here and brief me about this man Bishop. It'll take your mind off your daughter, won't it?'

He was a burly man, younger than me, but seeming infinitely older in wisdom and authority, with the strength which rested not only on his enormous muscle power. His hair was close-cropped to his large dome-shaped head; his face looked as if he'd shaved half an hour ago. Authority sat on those wide shoulders like a signature on a contract, fitted him as tailor-made as the dark blue suit he was wearing. Perversely I told myself it wasn't a grey lounge suit.

'Take your mind off your daughter, won't it, Inspector?'

'I suppose it will,' I grumbled.

He picked up a chair, twirled it round, and placed it backwards in front of me. When he squatted on it, I wondered the chair legs didn't bend. I told him everything I knew, everything I had thought, most of the things I had suspected, about Bishop. He asked very few questions but the few words he spoke drew information from me like a priest draws confession. He was an easy man to talk to, a sponge of a listener. I even told him about Nancy and my hopes for Bishop and her perhaps to get together, adding that it would help my domestic situation if they did. He smiled at that; 'I was married, once,' he said, and that established the right mood of sympathy though it didn't suggest further revelations.

He had been right; when I'd finished telling him what he wanted to know I realized my mind was at peace. The whole situation concerning my daughter had somehow fallen into perspective. I would have been a nuisance to Sarah, agitated the way I was. This way, she had a policewoman to hold her hand. I'd arrive there in peace and authority; we could discuss the matter calmly, and I could make the arrangements. Fortunately I belong to the Private Patients Plan; it costs a bit but is very good value for money. It would mean Helen could have a private ward when she came out of Intensive Care; we could visit her anytime, and the privilege wouldn't cost me a penny.

'Let's go and see Bishop,' he said.

Bishop was sitting in the armchair. When we came into interview room one, the animal fear look came to his face. The chief superintendent was bulky enough to inspire that; it was like travelling in the wake of a charging bull. But when he stopped, unlike the chief inspector he seemed to relax into a placid mound of gentleness.

He held out his hand. 'Hello, Mr Bishop,' he said, 'I'm Chief Detective Superintendent Arthur Pope from Scotland Yard. Don't let that bother you, you can call me anything you like.'

To my great surprise Bishop held out his hand, and though he flinched as he touched the chief superintendent's he shook it a couple of times before he took his hand back, as if he too had been mesmerized by the bulk of the man.

'I hope you can understand our difficulty,' Pope said.

For the first time I was able to be an audience and listen to his voice. It was mellifluous, smooth as cream. 'This story of yours is very hard to accept, you know. We hear many stories. We try always to listen to them but afterwards must come the logical process of whether we can believe them or not. I understand that Inspector Armstrong has listened to your story; he has reported it to me. I'm finding difficulty in grasping it. At this moment I have an open mind. *If* you have kidnapped Prince Charles, of course we shall have to give you a million pounds and send you on your way as you ask. If you haven't and you've made all this up just to engage our attention for a few hours then we shall have to see what we can do to help you. You can understand that, can't you?'

Bishop did not reply.

'I was just wondering if you could offer me a few more details. I mean it can't harm, can it, to tell us where and when you kidnapped the prince. I realize you can't tell us where you've put him, but it can't harm to let us know where you took him from. Was it outside the Palace? What did you do, get into his car?'

Being a spectator I had seen Bishop's withdrawal. I didn't know if Pope had seen it but it was there, as if a steel membrane had closed behind Bishop's eyes.

'I'm not going to talk to you, Mr Pope!' He turned and

beckoned me. 'That's the only man I'll talk to.'

I've never seen what happens when a charging bull runs against a concrete wall but I can imagine. Pope looked at me, looked back at Bishop, who had sat down again. He looked back at me, pawed the ground with his foot, sniffed the air, and blinked. 'What's that you say?' he asked, incredulously.

Bishop looked through and past him as if he were made of jelly. 'Inspector Armstrong,' he said, 'would you remind Mr Pope that within three hours and forty-five minutes Prince Charles will be dead.'

'*In* three hours and forty-five minutes you mean,' Pope barked, '*in* not *within*.' He was trying to assert himself but it didn't work. Bishop shrugged his shoulders. Pope took a half pace towards him but this time Bishop didn't flinch, didn't cower. All of a sudden Pope looked like a tired old British Army major trying to con a lady out of what was left of her jewellery. He looked shifty, fat, seedy. When he spoke his mellifluous voice had acquired a squeak.

'See here, my man!' he said. I could have laughed. The image was shattered. 'See here, my man! You're talking to me, Chief Detective Superintendent Pope from Scotland Yard! Now what's all this nonsense about kidnapping Prince Charles?'

Gone, gone! Bishop seemed to refocus his eyes so that he was actually looking at Pope and then something happened that any actor would give his billing to be able to do. I imagine it's the sort of thing Royal Personages like Prince Charles learn to do all the time. His eyes pulled focus on Chief Detective Superintendent Pope and it was as if Pope had never been there.

Pope turned to me. 'You've got a tough one here, haven't you?' he said, with forced joviality. 'You'd better get off to the hospital to see your wife.'

'With respect, Sir, I don't think he's going to talk to you. I've been with Mr Bishop four and a half hours now and I think he means what he says.'

'Then what do you suggest we do, man?' he snapped.

'As a detective *inspector* I suggest we launch an immediate and all-out attempt to verify his story once and for all.'

The chief superintendent looked at Bishop, looked at me, went to the door, opened it and called 'Sergeant.' Sergeant Jones bustled in carrying a clipboard and a ballpoint pen. 'Put him down,' the chief superintendent said, 'and book him. He's just wasting our time.' He turned to me. 'You get off to the hospital, Inspector. I'm surprised at you letting yourself be conned by a man like this.' He dusted his hands together symbolically. Somewhere inside himself he operated the pump that blew him back up to his former size and then he went out.

'Go gentle with him,' I said to the sergeant.

He nodded. 'I'll handle him like a baby!'

I went out of the interview room, saw the chief superintendent standing at the desk with the phone in his hand, obviously issuing a stream of orders. It would take a lot of them to redeem the rejection he'd just had. I turned the other way and sneaked up the back staircase. When I got to my office I closed the door behind me. Parkins had come back and Milner. Parkins was tapping at the typewriter and Milner was on the telephone.

Parkins looked up at me. 'Bloody paperwork,' he said, 'but I got a cough.' He'd been to Wandsworth Jail to interrogate a man who'd been given three years for shopbreaking. Parkins had traced him to another job, driving the car on a post office raid up the road.

'Did he name any names?' I asked.

'Honestly, my pad reads like a *Who's Who* of crime. He's given us the lot.'

'Lucky sod,' I said. 'It'll look good on your blotter.'

'Don't make any plans for tonight,' Milner said as he put the phone down. 'We're all out on a pick up, simultaneously. We're going to knock 'em all off at nine o'clock before they leave for work. I've just cancelled my date. You've drawn Paddy Michaels.'

'Hell. I hope you've given me six big coppers to take him with.'

He chuckled and reached for the phone again.

'Hang on,' I said, 'I've got to make an urgent call.' I spoke to the operator. It was the one who'd been snotty about the coffee. 'Can you find me the number of St Matthew's Hospital?' I asked.

She whined back at me. 'Isn't it time you've got a phone book up there? I mean, I'm very busy and looking up all these numbers doesn't make it easy. You ought to have a phone book!' She'd been looking up the number while she'd been complaining.

I asked for reception and they found Sarah immediately for me. 'You all right, love?' I said.

'I'm better now. That was very nice of you to send that policewoman. You *are* a thoughtful man.'

I felt like a heel. *I* ought to have thought of sending a policewoman. 'Look,' I said, 'I don't suppose there'll be any news for a while....'

'Oh yes, such a nice doctor's been out. Several times. He's been very good. It seems it's going all right. I told them, don't waste time coming out to talk to me, but he said it was all right.'

Relief flooded through me – relief, remorse that I was such an inadequate husband, and a great sense of love for Sarah for being such a wonderful wife. How many women would have been thoughtful enough to say that to the doctor?

'You're marvellous,' I said, 'and I love you.'

'She's going to be all right.' Her voice was soft and gentle but firm and full of authority. She should have interrogated Bishop! He'd have told Sarah everything we wanted to know.

'Look love, I've got a bad one at the moment. Would you mind if I stayed with it? I'll tell you all about it when I see you. But as long as Helen's all right and you're all right . . .?'

'Stay with your work,' she said. 'Honestly, there's nothing you can do here. I threw my nightie and toothbrush in to my bag and I've got a book with me.' She chuckled. 'I'll tell you something that'll make you laugh,' she said. 'I was a bit lost to know what to do about the boy when he comes home from school so I phoned up your Nancy. She's going to look after him and give him his dinner!'

'She's not *my* Nancy.' What a wonderful woman I'd married. At a time like that to be able to think of everything. I said a few things to her, conscious that Parkins and Milner were listening, then put the phone down. I picked it up again and asked for the switchboard supervisor. 'I have a lot of calls to make in a hurry and I don't want to mess around with Moaning Minnie all the time. Can you put somebody good on the board or handle it yourself?' I knew Alma. She loved to be connected to an investigation, however vicariously.

She was a little fat widow woman coming up to fifty with fingers like Medusa's snakes. She could dial a number faster than you could say it and I think she carried the whole of the London phone directory, all four volumes, in her head.

I spoke to the Palace first and told a lie. 'Chief Detective Superintendent Pope wants to verify where Prince Charles spent the night.'

The answer came back immediately.

CHAPTER FIVE

Lord Popham's butler answered the phone, refused to answer my question 'Did Prince Charles spend the night there?' He wasn't permitted to give out such information, not even to the police. Would I care to speak to His Lordship? Yes I would and damn quick. His Lordship had gone to the point-to-point meeting at Askrigg. His Lordship was doubtless available on the telephone of his car. Alma, bless her, must have been listening in, for when I depressed the button on the cradle to cut off the butler her voice came in.

'I have that number for you, Inspector. It's Miss Sally Bean. You know her. She's on television all the time.'

'Put her on.'

Sally Bean gurgled down the telephone. It took sixty vital seconds for me to stop the gurgle and get Lord Popham.

'Oh yes,' he drawled, 'went to the theatre, supper afterwards at Snaffles. Why do you ask? Did you want to know anything?'

Yes, I did want to know something, and in a hurry. 'Did Prince Charles spend the night with you?'

'I say, old boy, bit of a leading question, eh, what?'

I told another lie. 'I'm not an old boy, Your Lordship. With respect I'm speaking on behalf of Detective Chief Superintendent Pope.'

He wasn't impressed. I think if I'd said the Pope himself he wouldn't have been impressed either.

'Well, I mean to say, one doesn't like to lob out information to all and sundry. All sorts of stories get about, you know. Fuel for the fire, eh? So far as I know you are a voice on the telephone, aren't you? You could be William Hickey or somebody from *Private Eye*!' He guffawed and in the background I heard Sally Bean gurgling again, admiring his stupendous wit. He was right, of course.

'Is a constable anywhere near the car, Lord Popham? Could your chauffeur go and find one? He'll tell you who I am.' It was a gamble but it paid off.

'Well, if you put it like that, old boy, yes he did. I mean Prince Charles stayed the night at my place.'

'What time did he leave this morning?'

'I say, this isn't serious, is it?'

'Of course it is, or I wouldn't be asking all these questions.' I'd had too many of them weaving about in front of me in their lilac shirts and maroon bow ties, silkfaced evening dress jackets stained with champagne, a glassy look in their eyes. I'd pulled too many of the out of crashed Jensens and Healeys and Lamborghinis, pissed out of their skulls.

My voice must have come as a cold douche to him for when he spoke his voice had assumed a crisp and serious tone. 'He left at half past seven,' he said. 'He was going sailing for the day with Lord Wentworth from Chatham. They wanted to miss the early morning rush.'

'*They?*'

'His detective also slept at the flat. The butler has a guest room. Funny thing though. We have a private underground car park. When I went down there at half past nine Prince Charles's car was still there.'

'Can you get into the car park without leaving the building?'

'No, that's a disadvantage. You have to walk round into the mews.'

'You saw or heard nothing unusual?'

'No, nothing at all. I say, seriously, is there anything wrong?'

'Nothing at all,' I said. 'It's purely an internal police matter.'

'Don't tell me the detective's fiddling his expenses?' He guffawed again. I hated to malign a fellow officer but it was the one way to stop the question quickly. 'Something like that,' I said, 'but I'm not at liberty to say any more.'

Telephone down, telephone up. 'The nearest police station to Lord Popham's home.' She connected me at once. This time I identified myself with my own name and rank. 'Have you a car in the vicinity of Billing Mews?' I asked when I got through to their radio room. My good luck held.

'One parked right outside.'

'Could you ask them to drive in to the underground private garage there. They'll find Prince Charles's car. Ask them to look at it. Can you cross hatch the telephone?' Three clicks later I was talking directly to the police car as it nosed its way into the garage down a ramp. A voice from the library attached to the radio room came on the line, identifying Prince Charles's car number. The co-driver said, 'Got it.'

'Right, we're parked next to it. What are we looking for?'

'I don't know.'

I heard the click as the telephone was handed over.

'Driver here, Constable Bailey. I'm going to back the police car away. Constable Little is looking in through the near-side window. He's turned; he's put his thumb up. I think that means the key is in the ignition. This type of garage they usually leave the key in. Now he's put his hand on the door handle, now he's taken it off again. He's crouched on the floor looking under the car. He's stood up again, he's put his hand on the handle, he's pressed the handle, opened the door. Well, that's a relief anyway. Now he's looking into the car. He's put his head inside the car, he's looking under the dashboard. I think he's pulled the bonnet catch. Yes, he's walked round to the front of the car and he's lifted up the bonnet. He's shaking his head. Nothing in there that he can see. Ah, now he's making a sign at me. Now he's shouting. Do you want the car started, Inspector?'

'Yes, please.'

I heard him shout 'yes', his voice echoing round the garage. Then I heard the sound of another engine. There was a silence. I heard the engine accelerate and decelerate again. A silence again broken by the other constable's voice.

'The car seems to be perfectly all right, Inspector, in perfect working order. What do you want us to do now?'

'Nothing,' I said, 'and thank you very much indeed.'

'Think nothing of it, Inspector, all in a day's work.'

So it was, but I would have had a hard job explaining if that car had had a bomb planted in it.

There comes a time in any investigation when, somehow, the facts before you become less significant than your own inner conviction. How many times had I stood listening to a witness writing down the perfectly reasonable statement they were making about their part in events, when suddenly I'd reached a quite illogical conclusion that what they were telling me was a fabrication. Call it sixth sense, call it what you will, but it existed, it was real. I'd had that feeling since the first moment I'd started to talk to Bishop. I had that feeling now as I asked myself – why wouldn't Prince Charles use his car? There were many logical explanations. Possibly Lord Wentworth had sent a car for him. Possibly that car had been waiting outside Lord Popham's when the prince came out with his detective. Possibly the prince didn't feel like driving this morning. These were all *possibilities*. But I was not convinced.

How did Bishop know as much as he did about the prince's movements? How did he know what clothes the prince was wearing? That he was going to Chatham to sail Lord Wentworth's yacht for the day? Of course, he could have found out all this information, but he wasn't the sort to undertake even such a simple investigation, to assemble facts of that sort. People wouldn't talk easily to him; they'd be suspicious of his motives.

I rang the Palace again. Used Pope's rank and name again. They gave me the extension in Scotland Yard that deals with the officers who guard Royalty. 'What's the name of the man looking after Prince Charles?'

They told me.

'Have you heard from him today?'

Quick look at the files. 'Yes.'

'When? Where from?'

Let it be Chatham! Let it be Lord Wentworth's yacht!

'0645 hrs. Lord Popham's flat. They were just leaving . . .'

'. . . to spend the day sailing on Lord Wentworth's yacht.'

'That's right.'

'Any mention of transport?'

'Hang on, I'll look again.' Rustle of papers. 'No mention of transport. By that, I mean no requests for transport aid or surveillance.' I knew that sometimes, if a Royal person were going somewhere 'sensitive', like through an area where pickets were out, a police car and/or motor bicycles were provided as outriders.

'When do you expect to hear again?'

'Not until this evening. We have the directions for the yacht radio in case of emergency.' They'd need that, wouldn't they? The King is Dead, long live the King! Succession to the throne is instant, and presumably the heir to the throne must, at all times, be accessible.

I was getting nothing but negatives. Every step I took should have persuaded me that everything in the life of the prince was proceeding naturally, that there was no connection between Bishop and Prince Charles, that all Bishop wanted was, as the chief superintendent had said, to engage our attention for a few hours. If only he could have given us *one* fact he couldn't have known unless his story were true. *One* fact. Hastily I reviewed everything he'd said to me. It wasn't much and running it through my mind didn't take long.

Milner came across the office, perched on the edge of my desk. 'I heard about your daughter. They'll look after her all right, you know.'

'Thanks,' I said, ashamed to confess I hadn't been thinking about Helen.

'What are you working on at the moment?' he asked. We tend to talk about our cases in the office, to compare notes and opinions. It helps, sometimes, to get a fresh slant on things. I couldn't discuss Bishop with him. A simple man, he wouldn't understand. He's a man who likes to follow the rules and he'd have obeyed Detective Chief Superintendent Pope without question.

'Nothing important. Just checking a couple of leads. Probably nothing in it.'

'I've just taken Lil downstairs. I'm damn sure she's running a call-girl racket as well as that model agency of hers. You wouldn't like to go down and lean on her for me, would you? Put on your tough act?'

Normally I would have gone down into the cells and made a noise, acting tough. Milner could then come down and play it gentle. It's amazing how many women will give you a cough after such a treatment.

'I can't at the moment,' I said, 'but later on I might find some time. . . .'

He was put out, I could see that. We all help each other and I wasn't being very cooperative.

'If you're too *busy*,' he said and took his arse off my desk. Hell, I wasn't too busy.

'I'll go down there,' I said, 'give her a hard time for you. . . .'
'Not too hard. . . .'
'Get her ready for your soft and sympathetic approach. . . .'
I would have gone down, too, but the telephone rang.
'Sergeant Jones here, Inspector. We're ready to charge Bishop.'
'So soon?'
'We thought you'd like to get it over with.'
'I'll be right down.'

Milner was sitting on Parkins's desk, and both were looking at me.

'I've just got to charge somebody,' I said, 'and then I'll look in on Lil. What are you holding her on?'

'Suspected possession of stolen property. . . .'

'And you want to find out about the call-girl racket, eh?'

'That's right. But only if you can spare the time. . . .' His sarcasm didn't escape me.

They'd brought Bishop out of the cells and put him back in interview room one. He seemed at home in there. Sergeant Jones, the chief inspector, Constables Milton and Semple, and me. It was an impressive array of might. As soon as I came in, the chief picked up the clipboard on which Jones had placed the documentation. The Legal Department must have put their skates on to get it completed so quickly. The chief read the preamble, naming everybody there, quoting the Judges' Rules about Bishop not being forced to say anything but anything he did say would be taken down. . . . I stood silent, listening and looking.

Bishop was absolutely still, at a sort of military attention with his feet together, gnarled hands down the seams of his trousers. You could tell that, once, he'd been a soldier. Once he'd stood like that but his interrogators had quoted no Judges' Rules at him. Now he'd got what he wanted, a sense of belonging. He'd come up in front of a magistrate who'd doubtless warn him, sentence him but then suspend the sentence. It'd be a four day charade, but during that time, perhaps Bishop would see sense. Anyway, he'd hold the centre of the stage for four days and that should be enough to keep him happy for a while.

He must have felt my eyes on him. He swivelled his look

away from the chief inspector to me. The chief inspector droned on, while Semple took down each word in shorthand.

Bishop spoke. His words didn't come out loud, and Semple merely glanced up and then decided not to make a note of the mumbling. Only I heard the words, but they were directed at me.

'Prince Charles is wearing a green tie with a red stripe. The stripe has a navy blue edge to it.'

The chief inspector stopped. 'Did you want to say something?' he said to Bishop. 'You'll get your chance to speak when I've finished.'

Bishop, smiling at me, shook his head slowly.

'I didn't get what he said, Sir,' Semple said.

'It doesn't matter,' the chief inspector said, steamrollering on.

But it did matter. My mind was doing mathematical handsprings. How many colours of ties are there? Say six. How many colours of stripe are there? Say another six. That's thirty-six combinations. And how many colours of edging could there be? Say six again, that's two hundred and sixteen. Bishop had one chance in two hundred he could be right. Perhaps he could have guessed the grey lounge suit but you don't guess one colour combination in two hundred. Now I had the bit of hard factual matter that I could use to put his case out of my mind forever. Now I could lay this ghost to rest, this whispering shade that nagged me and said 'perhaps Bishop might be telling the truth!'

I itched for the chief inspector to finish but Rules are Rules, Procedure is Procedure and the British Legal System ensures a man has every chance when the police accuse him. The Judges' Rules load the dice against the police and in favour of the suspect; Bishop didn't take advantage of any of his opportunities. He said nothing except to answer 'yes' when necessary. The whole puppet show took thirty minutes and after it I raced into interview room two. I couldn't bear Milner and Parkins's cynical eyes on me again. Alma re-connected me quickly with Lord Popham's car. I had to wait four minutes while they fetched him from a horsebox. When he came on the radio telephone his voice was quite crisp.

'I hope you're not going to turn out to be a nuisance, Inspector?' he said.

'One question only. You may not think it's important but please try to answer accurately. What colour tie is Prince Charles wearing today?'

I had expected him to say, 'You must be out of your mind,' but he didn't. No doubt determined to get rid of me as quickly as possible.

'Green.'

'Plain green or a pattern?'

'I'll have to think.' He thought. The airwaves were heavy with effort.

'I seem to remember some kind of stripe,' he said. 'Oh yes, I remember. He's wearing the old Carpathian tie.'

'And what colour is that, Lord Popham?'

'It's green, of course, with a red stripe and a very delicate blue edge. It's rather nice actually.' He put down the phone without saying goodbye, no doubt determined I wouldn't get in a second question.

I went up to the chief inspector's room. I'm a gambler who risks everything on one throw. I'd never make money on the horses. On the few occasions I have a flutter like on the Derby, I pick one horse and put a pound on its nose to win. I've no time for each-way betting. I've never won on the Derby yet. I risked everything on one throw.

'I know you're sick to death at the sound of Bishop's name, Chief Inspector, and frankly so am I, but will you indulge me in just one last thing. Then I promise you I'll forget all about it.'

'One last thing, eh? It's a deal. What is it?'

'Ring Detective Chief Superintendent Pope at Scotland Yard!'

His eyebrows climbed to the top of his head. 'And get myself made inspector again? It's taken me a long time to earn this desk, you know! What do I say to him when I ring him? I know damn well what he'll say to me!'

I smiled, anticipating the explosion that had to come. 'Ask him what colour Inspector Parkins's tie is. . . .'

The explosion didn't come; the request was so outrageous that not even he thought I was serious. He started to laugh, a long low rumble that came from somewhere near his balls and erupted like lava out of Vesuvious.

'One thing I must say for you, Armstrong,' he said, wiping the tears out of his eyes, 'you always manage to come up with the unexpected. Ask him what colour Inspector Parkins's tie is, eh? I won't even ask you why and what's more I think I'll do it! They'll never believe me when I tell them.'

I could see him in the coffee room the senior officers used. I could see them pissing themselves rolling about on the carpet.

He got Pope first try, putting his phone on the loudspeaker circuit so that I could hear for myself the eruption he expected from the chief superintendent. Oddly enough none came.

'This has to be some kind of inverted logic,' Pope said, 'probably a bit of that lateral thinking we hear so much about today. Like the dwarf who can't reach the lift button for the twelfth floor. All right, I'll play. Parkins is a detective inspector; he's either wild or conservative. I don't know the man. I will guess he's conservative. He's at work today presumably so I'll stick my neck out and guess he's wearing a sports coat and flannels. All right, he's wearing a grey tie, with a blue stripe on it. Anything else?'

The chief inspector looked at me and I shook my head.

'Not for the moment, Chief Superintendent,' he said, 'I'll get back to you later.'

'Now ring Parkins,' I said, 'and ask him what colour tie he's wearing.' I knew it was a navy blue tie with a white check pattern. It looked horrible with his green jacket.

'Right,' the chief inspector said, after he'd talked to Parkins. 'We now have two facts and presumably you're going to connect them.'

'When you were charging Bishop he said "Prince Charles was wearing a green tie with a red stripe with a blue edging on it." I've talked to Lord Popham. . . .'

The chief inspector threw up his hands in horror but didn't interrupt me.

'Lord Popham has seen Prince Charles today, and confirmed that Prince Charles is wearing exactly that colour of tie; if you don't believe me the switchboard will connect you with Lord Popham, who's at the Askrigg point-to-point right now with a radio telephone in his car.'

That stopped the chief dead. He looked at me as if trying to read my thoughts. 'You're not pulling my leg, are you? No, you wouldn't be.'

'I'll save you some mathematics, Chief. It's at least one in two hundred he could get the colour of the tie right. You saw how wrong Detective Chief Superintendent Pope was. . . .'

I will say this for him; when he moves he moves quickly. He picked up the telephone and got on to Pope right away. He told him about the tie. Pope said, 'Put him on. You're absolutely sure,' he said to me, 'that's what Bishop said while they were charging him?'

'Absolutely certain.' I told him the rest of it, about Popham having seen the prince this morning, the detective having phoned in, the car still lying in the garage.

'I'm coming back.'

'With respect, Chief Supintendent, I don't think he'll talk to you and there isn't a lot of time left.'

'I'm not going to ask him to talk to me. You can handle that side of it, I'll do the rest. Are you there, Chief Inspector?'

'Yes.'

'We'll need a radio room, a clean switchboard. You know the details. I'll put out a Red alert from here.'

'You're taking it seriously then, Sir?'

'We have no alternative.'

I went downstairs, saw Sergeant Jones. 'Bring Bishop up and put him in interview room one,' I said, 'and give him a cup of tea.'

It would be five minutes before they arrived. I used two of them to phone Sarah and hear there was no change. When Bishop arrived I was waiting for him. Oddly enough, I'd ceased to regard him as a criminal.

'There's a chance you might get your million pounds,' I said, 'but you'll have to cooperate. We've started a full-scale investigation. As soon as we can prove that Prince Charles is missing, you'll get your money. Knowing the way they work the first thing they'll do is send a psychiatrist to prove you're not crazy. You'll have to cooperate with him, too.'

I had guessed correctly who the psychiatrist would be. Professor Sir William Dolbey. Harley Street. Guy's Hospital. He is a small affable man who wears a navy blue suit with a white pinstripe, a snowy white shirt, a silver tie without stripes, horn-rimmed glasses, almost bald. He looks like a stockbroker. They brought him in a police car.

'Quite exciting,' he said, 'riding along with the hooter blowing. Now where is this chap and what can you tell me about him?'

I told him what little I knew and stressed there was very little time.

'I talked to them on the telephone in the police car, they did say it was a matter of some urgency. Don't worry, I shan't let him ramble on.' He chuckled jovially, patted my arm as if I were Bishop's father.

'How shall we work it?' I asked.

'Will he talk to me?'

'I think he will.'

'Well, just in case, you come along inside. If he makes an issue of not talking to me let him chatter to you a bit.'

'What sort of things?'

'It would help if you can get him on to his attitudes. You know the sort of thing, controversial questions. Does he vote Conservative or Labour? What does he think of Enoch Powell? Was Che Guevara a hero or a blackguard? Don't take any notice of me.'

We went inside together and I introduced them. Sir William made no attempt to shake hands.

'Are you going to talk to me or to the inspector?'

'I'll talk to either one of you,' Bishop said, 'as long as it will convince you I'm not crazy.'

'We're all a little bit crazy, you know,' Sir William said. 'What do you think is crazy?'

'A man who comes in here and says he's kidnapped Prince Charles.'

'Have you?' I was surprised by the directness of the question. And so, apparently, was Bishop. He smiled at Sir William in a lazy kind of way, as if Sir William's sanity were in question, not his own. I was amazed by the speed at which the two of them reached an understanding. I suppose it was part of Sir William's training as a psychiatrist, to be able quickly to establish an atmosphere in which the conversation could take place.

And that's all it was, or so it seemed to me: a normal conversation between acquaintances, an exchange of points of view that could have taken place in a pub over a couple of half-pints of beer.

I could see no reason for most of the dialogue; the questions seemed to be leading nowhere. I felt like a judge when a barrister wanders all round the point, but I had no gavel with which to rap the Bench. I had to sit there, fuming inside myself at what I took to be a waste of valuable time. I'm used to interrogations, of course. It's part of the stock in trade of any good copper. And of course, come to think of it, our questioning always led to finding factual information, whereas Sir William was probing an atmosphere, a state of mind, without regard for the truth or untruth of any matters of fact. Each time he managed to bring the conversation round to this question of Prince Charles, and the possible kidnapping, but after the failure of his first question to elicit a direct answer, each time he skirted round it. I longed to look at my watch, to make some gesture that would remind him how little time we had, but didn't want to upset the delicate balance he had so quickly established between them. Bishop, for his part, was totally relaxed. He'd started off like a small boy who thinks he's going to fail the end of term test, but gradually his confidence returned when he found he could answer the questions.

At last, Sir William asked him again, point-blank, directly, 'Have you kidnapped him?'

'Yes, I have.'

'Why did you do that?'

'Because I was short of money. I'm always short of money.'

'That's not Prince Charles's fault, is it?'

'He has plenty of money.'

'He has a lot of responsibilities too. Anyway, why pick on him?'

'Because I knew you wouldn't let a man like that stay kidnapped. I mean, if it was somebody ordinary...'

'Like Inspector Armstrong here. Is he ordinary? Is he what you think of as somebody ordinary?'

'No, he's a policeman. Policemen aren't ordinary.'

'Policemen are pigs, eh?'

'I didn't say that.' A crafty smile came on Bishop's face. 'The police are meant to protect us, aren't they?'

'Do you really think that? What about black policemen?'

'They're all policemen, no matter what colour they are.'

'What about Prince Charles? Would he make a good king?'

'I've never thought about it.'

'Well, think about it. Seems a nice lad to me. What about you?'

'He's all right. If you have to have a king I suppose he's as good as anybody.'

'Would you rather have a president?'

'After Watergate?'

'What about Rule by Committee, a bureaucracy?'

'You mean office workers running the country? Civil servants? All the bother of my life has been caused by office workers. They can't understand what it's like for men like me.'

'Anyone in particular?'

'The whole lot of them.'

'Given you a bad time, have they?'

'You could say that again.'

I took a chance on interrupting. 'Has Mr Jackson given you a bad time?' Jackson was the only name I'd learned from Bishop's life. It seemed worth asking a specific question. Sir William had taken his handkerchief from the cuff of his immaculate shirt. He brought it to his face as if to blow his nose. But he made no sound.

'Not really,' Bishop said, looking at Sir William play with the handkerchief. 'It's the system, really, not the individual men in it. They do their best, but the system doesn't allow them any individuality.'

'Let me ask you one last question,' Sir William said when he had put away the handkerchief, 'and then we'll leave you in peace. Do you think one man ever has the right to take the life of another man? Let's imagine you were looking down the sights of a rifle and you'd drawn a bead on, let's say, Adolf Hitler. Would you pull the trigger?'

Bishop didn't need to think about that one. Or perhaps he was trying to supply the answers he thought Sir William required of him. Frankly, I couldn't see which were the important questions, which the unimportant ones. That's part of the technique of a psychiatric investigation, I suppose. To cloak the loaded questions in a lot of innocent verbiage.

'Yes, I would,' Bishop said.

Sir William got up from the chair in which he'd been sitting. He pulled out a slim gold hunter watch and looked at it. 'Drink your tea before it turns cold, Mr Bishop,' he said.

Bishop looked cheekily across the room at him.

'*Am* I crazy, Sir William?' he asked.

Sir William smiled back at him, without any hint of patronizing or humouring him. 'That's the 64-thousand-dollar question.'

Bishop matched smile for smile. 'With the one million pound answer,' he said.

CHAPTER SIX

Bishop settled back in his chair; Sir William and I left the room together. We stood in the corner away from the desk.

'I understand you're to be the liaison officer,' he said. 'That's a good thing. Bishop has formed an attachment to you.'

'Has he? It doesn't show.'

'It does if you know where to look.'

'And the other matter. The question of his being crazy or not. I suppose that shows, too?'

He ignored my question. 'You've given me a difficult problem,' he said, 'and not much time to cope with it. Whether the man is *crazy* or not doesn't matter at the moment. We have to assess if he's *believable*. We could simply hold him while you make the necessary inquiries to discover if Prince Charles is missing or not. Presumably there would be no problem to find a large yacht at sea in a busy waterway. But, of course, all the time you are looking, the clock is ticking, and if the prince *is* missing, you may run out of time before you can verify that fact. Therefore we come to the question, is Bishop believable? I'm afraid the answer to that question must be yes, he is believable. I can't say if he has actually kidnapped Prince Charles or not. It would take many hours of quite intensive work to uncover that. But he is *believable* and for the time being, we must take him seriously.'

Chief Detective Superintendent Pope emerged from interview room two. When he saw us, he held open the door and we went in. No time had been lost. Three sergeants were sitting at three desks in the room. The door between interview room two and the station radio room had been taken off its hinges. Three extra tables had been brought in, and on each table were two telephones. On the far side of the room was a bench, and at the bench two policewomen sat each side of a telephone switchboard. A man in black overalls was finishing the connections to the back of the switchboard. I noticed that, in place of the usual pencil, he had a long thin screwdriver tucked behind his ear. To the left of the room, a door led into interview room one. Like all doors in this part of the building, it was soundproof. The last remaining space was taken up with a desk for Pope, which closed the gap between two of the other three desks. On Pope's desk were four telephones and a radio microphone on a stand. Sir William was given Pope's chair; Pope and I sat on the desk top. I felt like Tweedledee.

Sir William repeated the substance of what he had said to me: that Bishop was believable. 'I can give you three definite results,' Sir William said. 'If you don't mind, at this juncture I won't go into the thinking behind my analysis since that would merely waste your time. I imagine all you're interested in are the results?'

Pope nodded.

'Right. Firstly, Bishop *is* mentally disturbed. The effect of this, so far as you are concerned, is that you can expect some irrationality. It's quite on the cards that he'll talk to Inspector Armstrong here but not to you or anyone else. If he has such an attitude, he will persist in it, even though it could mean the loss of his primary objective, to gain a million pounds. You realize, of course, that the money is quite insignificant to him as money? He's solely concerned with the independence from officialdom the money would buy. Frankly, a thousand pounds would serve just as well.'

'So we could bargain with him?'

'On the contrary. You must not try to bargain. The sum of one million pounds, because it has no mathematical value for him, has become a symbol. If you bargain, you destroy that symbol. No, I'm afraid that, if the worst comes to the worst and he has got Prince Charles, you'll have to find one million pounds. No more, no less. For example, he could react quite violently if even *one* pound were missing! Secondly, Bishop is a solitary man. He has no one to trust. He therefore trusts no one, nothing. You will have to give him his million pounds in actual money. You'll have to let him walk out of here on his own. Please understand this quite clearly. He trusts no one, and nothing. At the moment he has conceived a certain love for Inspector Armstrong. . . .'

I shifted uncomfortably on the desk top. Sir William gave

small smile. 'That embarrasses you, doesn't it?'

'I suppose it does. . . . I'm not one of *them*. . . .'

'Yours is the normal reaction. But do try to remember what I have said in your dealings with this man. Try to remember that this man *loves* you, and will behave towards you as emotionally and irrationally as any lover would do. . . .'

'I hope he's not going to start calling me sweetie. . . .'

'Love and sex don't always have to be associated,' he said wearily, 'but we won't go off on that particular tangent.'

I felt suitably rebuked, especially seeing Pope glare at me.

'Now we come to the most important thing,' Sir William said. 'It seems to me, even on such a short acquaintance, that Bishop has no respect for human life. To judge from what you said about him being a prisoner of war and what was done to him, I would say he has accepted the philosophy that death is inevitable and the date and time and method of it is irrelevant. This means, of course, that he would have no qualms on moral grounds about kidnapping Prince Charles, and about leaving him somewhere to die.'

The pattern was quite clear. He said he'd done it, he could have done it, and we had to believe for the moment that he might have done it.

'Let me ask you one question, Sir William,' Pope said. 'At this present moment, is it your professional opinion that an investigation into this matter is justified?'

Sir William got up. 'If you didn't conduct a most thorough investigation into all aspects of this matter, I would think you derelict in your duties as a police officer,' he said, 'and that is what I intend to say in my report to the commissioner.'

'Thank you very much,' Pope said.

I didn't know if he was thanking Sir William for clearing him with his boss, but we all like to protect ourselves wherever possible. The higher you get, I suppose, the more important it becomes.

Sir William left the office.

'Right,' Pope said, 'let's get on with it. We've no time at all.'

We had barely three hours left, if Bishop were telling the truth. I checked myself. I must not think like that. I must accept that Bishop could be, and therefore was, telling the truth. It was an awesome thought.

Pope used his microphone to talk to Commissioner Bailey, who presumably was sitting on the high-ranking equivalent of tentertooks. He quoted Sir William's exact words, a remarkable feat of memory since he'd taken no notes.

I spoke to one of the sergeants.

'I'm David MacLaren, Inspector,' he said, 'but I answer to the name of Jock.'

I told Jock about Bishop being employed by a Cleaning Company. 'It's worth starting by finding out which Cleaning Company has the contract for Lord Popham's building, in Billing Crescent.'

He was saved a job. Harry Ritchie came in. 'I took care of that little matter for you, Inspector,' he said. 'If you've got a minute.'

I took him to Pope, explained that I'd sent him out to check on Bishop. Harry had brought back as complete a history as we'd get. Apparently, the building in which Bishop lived was owned by an old lady, a Mrs Calleja, who had no one to talk to. She'd let Bishop stay virtually rent free and seemed to have spent most of her recent life trying to talk to him. I could guess she hadn't got many answers, but what she had, Harry had extracted from her.

Bishop had lived there, on and off, for four years. In one basement room. Harry had even been in the room, which he said was neat and tidy. It contained a thousand books, all much-used paperbacks. Mrs Calleja confirmed that Bishop had been in and out of employment. He couldn't, as she put it, settle to a job. Always the name Jackson kept cropping up. Jackson apparently had been round to the house several times. Once or twice, he'd even stayed the night. Mrs Calleja described him as a nondescript sort of man. No personality. No drive. Apparently she liked men with a bit of fire in them. That, she'd told Harry, was why she'd married a Spaniard. He was now dead. According to her, Bishop had 'fire' in him. Every time he quit a job he came back to Arlington Villas with fire in him. 'She's a go-er,' Harry explained. 'Even though she must be touching seventy-five she told me she likes men, especially my age. . . .'

'You were lucky to get out of there alive,' Pope said, revealing his human side at last.

'At the moment, Bishop's employed by the Sparkle Cleaning Company. "Bring Sparkle into your Lives" – that's their slogan, would you believe it?'

'Try the Sparkle Cleaning Company,' I called across to Jock. 'Ask them if they have the contract for Lord Popham's.'

'Bishop kept disappearing,' Harry continued. 'Sometimes he'd be away for a night; once he was away for four nights. When he came back, he was always bad-tempered for a while.'

'A girlfriend?' Pope asked.

'It sounded that way. Mrs Calleja didn't have any details, though apparently she tried to pump him several times.'

'A girlfriend sounds unlikely,' I said.

'Unless she was somebody as afflicted as he was.'

'Blind, perhaps? Couldn't see his scars.'

While we were concentrating on Bishop, the other desk was trying to make contact with Prince Charles. Now they had all the coastguard stations at the mouth of the Thames looking for him. No one had seen the yacht. It was no longer moored off Chatham.

They found the resident manager of the yacht club, and put him on the telephone, crossed to the radio/loudspeaker on Pope's desk top.

'Yes, Lord Wentworth did have his yacht here. He was using one of our guest moorings. You know, we find it a very good idea to keep a few moorings for a certain type of guest. . . .'

'I imagine you do.' Pope's voice was crisp and precise as he broke in. 'Is the yacht there now?'

'Oh no! It left. Rather strange. We didn't know. . . .'

'When did it leave . . .?'

'This morning. . . . I said to myself, what a lovely sight. . . .'

'Who was on it?'

'I couldn't say. You see, when I woke up – I always wake about five o'clock, seems I can't stay in bed after that time . . .'

'What time did it sail?'

'I was coming to that, Constable, what did you say your name was . . .?'

'I'm not a constable any more. I happen to be a chief superintendent and I apologize in advance if I should happen to sound rude but I'm most anxious to get specific information about that yacht. Would you mind awfully if I asked a few questions and you answered yes or no?'

'Well, really, if that's the way you go about things. . . .'

'It is, Mr Partridge, but only, I assure you, when we're in a hurry. Did you see the boat leave?'

'I can't answer yes or no to that. I did NOT see the boat leave its mooring. I DID see the boat leave the basin.'

'Did you see who was on it?'

'I did see someone in the cockpit, someone in the bows, but I could not identify them. I imagine that's what you want to know. Did I identify them?'

'You're perfectly right, Mr Partridge. Did you?'

'No.'

'Why not?'

'Because they were too far away.'

'You didn't form any impression who they might be?' I could understand Pope's reluctance to say – was it Prince Charles? The gossip would be round the yacht club within minutes.

'The man on the tiller could have been Lord Wentworth. I've no idea who the others might have been.'

'Others? There were others?'

'Yes.'

'How many?' Pope said, managing to hide his exasperation.

'Two.'

'And you've no idea, no impression of who they might be?'

'They were both male, I would say.'

That was something.

'You see, Chief Superintendent, I was out myself. In my *Vivacity*. I've been having quite a bit of weather helm with her and I've changed the rigging. That was why I couldn't sleep. It'd been on my mind, what with the race coming on Saturday. I wanted to find out if I'd cured the weather helm. So I took her out this morning. It was clear at first, but then the mist came in, and visibility was down to a few hundred yards. As I was coming back in, the other yacht passed me. It was on the fringes of the mist. It could have been Lord Wentworth's yacht, I'm not absolutely certain of that, but it was the only other yacht out at that time, and when I got back in I found Lord

Wentworth's yacht had left its mooring. Which is a pity, because I wanted him to sign the visitor's book, which we keep in the club house, since we rebuilt it last year after the fire. . . .'

Pope switched off the loudspeaker. 'Say goodbye to him when he finishes, Mary, will you?' he asked.

Peter, the sergeant on the desk near the radio room, had started contacting the coastguard points, probing farther down the river. I was working it out in my mind. If the yacht had left at eight o'clock it had already been sailing for eight hours or more. It could be anywhere in that time. Where was it heading? A round trip and back to the yacht club? Or were they headed back to the permanent mooring off Cowes? Were they sailing or motoring?

'Listen to this,' Peter said ominously. Mary plugged the voice through to the loudspeaker. It was slow and precise, a country voice. 'Would you say that again,' Peter said into his telephone.

The voice came over the speaker. 'It's not the day to go looking for someone out there. No, sir, it is not! Because for why? Because the mist is rolling in, that's for why, and the wind, she's dropped something cruel, and many's the boat out there's languishing in the calm. . . .'

'Tell him this isn't the B.B.C. and a Book at Bedtime,' Pope said.

'What's the forecast, Coxswain?' Peter asked quickly.

'No wind, none to speak of hardly at all, and then the fog might be coming down, but then again, she might not.'

'Get us a proper weather forecast,' Pope said irritably, 'but not from Captain Bligh. . . .'

The weather forecast was bad; unsettled, wind dropping, mist and possible fog.

'If Prince Charles is on that boat,' Pope said, 'I hope he's got an anorak with him. And a warm sweater.'

'They're bound to have a motor on the yacht,' I said, digging into my scant knowledge of seafaring craft.

'A motor is not much good if you can't see where you're going. In any case, in weather like this it'll be throttled back. Remember they are in the middle of one of the busiest sea lanes in the world.'

Pope pressed his microphone key and spoke directly to the

commissioner, reporting what we'd discovered about the wind and weather.

'I've been on to the Palace,' the commissioner said. 'We've had to tell them everything. They won't like the weather report.' The line went dead.

Pope grabbed my arm. 'Come next door,' he said.

Sir William had waited in the corridor outside and Pope conferred with him. Sir William thought for a moment. 'I think you might have an idea,' he said.

Pope wanted to bring Bishop fully into the picture. But he wanted to do it with the psychiatrist standing by and, of course, me there. It seemed novel to me, but having novel ideas which work is the way you get to be a chief superintendent.

We went into interview room one. Pope ignored Bishop and threw open the connecting doors. These rooms had been designed for just such an emergency, so that the three rooms could work as one suite in case of a large-scale emergency. Jock and his colleague carried Pope's desk through; the radio electronics man had allowed sufficient length of lead to be able to bring in the microphone, the loudspeaker, and all four telephones. They placed the desk where Pope could see down the length of the three rooms; his commanding voice could be heard everywhere.

I watched Bishop. He seemed delighted, even amused by these preparations. He would be of course; *he* had been the one to originate them and that would flatter any man's ego.

Sir William seated himself in the other armchair, making a church steeple of his fingers. He didn't appear to be looking anywhere in particular; one could have believed him to be half asleep. I guessed otherwise. He had already impressed me enormously.

'We've talked to Mrs Calleja,' I said to Bishop, 'and we know you're employed by the Sparkling Cleaning Company.'

Pope had a sudden thought and shouted down the rooms. 'Send a car for that man Jackson, Jock,' he ordered, 'and have him brought here.'

'Jackson can't tell anything,' Bishop said, 'nor can Mrs Calleja.'

'She told us you have a girlfriend,' I replied.

Bishop laughed. 'That's about on a par with the rest of the

information you'll get from her,' he said.

'She said she'd been letting him live rent free so he owes some kind of loyalty to her, you'd think,' Pope said irascibly, still talking to me as if Bishop weren't there.

'She let me live in a room nobody else would have wanted. I kept the room clean and tidy. If I hadn't been there the rats would have moved in. If anybody owes anybody she owes me.'

That was logical. Unkind but logical. I glanced at Sir William and caught a slight nod; he thought it was logical too.

Pope brought his chair and placed it midway between where I was sitting and Sir William. Bishop was to the right and slightly in front of him but Pope continued to ignore him completely. 'Let's turn our thinking inside out,' Pope said. He wanted to bounce his ideas off me with Sir William as umpire, ready to throw the ball back if it should happen to bounce out of the court. 'One half of our effort is employed trying to locate Prince Charles on a boat. We know they're going to have a difficult job because of the weather and the fact that Lord Wentworth's yacht radio, for whatever reason, doesn't seem to be working and we can't get through on the radio telephone. You could say that part of us doesn't believe Bishop's story. I think the other half of us should now completely accept Bishop's story. The problem becomes as follows. Bishop has kidnapped Prince Charles. Prince Charles is the future monarch of this country. Bishop has arranged matters so that if we don't give him a million pounds and release him without surveillance within a stated time Prince Charles will die. There isn't much time left. We therefore have to start planning what we are going to do. We cannot let Prince Charles die. I think we're all agreed on that?'

'Do you want me to play Devil's Advocate?' Sir William asked. 'I agree with everything you've said so far; I think you've taken a very logical approach; but we cannot necessarily accept that everyone agrees about saving the life of our future monarch. For example, one or two Members of Parliament wouldn't agree. . . .'

'I didn't want to get into political thinking,' Pope said.

'Nor do I, because that would waste valuable time. But it would help in your approach to this problem if you accept that some people may have no interest in saving Prince Charles. You should include Mr Bishop among those people.'

As distinct from Pope, Sir William turned and acknowledged Bishop as he used his name. Now it was Bishop's turn to nod his head.

'Point taken,' Pope said, 'and thank you very much.' He got up and went to his desk. Without sitting down he pressed the button that activated his microphone. 'A thought occurs to me, Commissioner,' he said. 'That million pounds. Where do we get it?'

'We're already on to that. I was going to ask you if there are any special requirements?'

Without letting go of the key Pope spoke to me, scrupulously avoiding looking at Bishop. 'Do you know if there are special requirements, Inspector Armstrong?' he said.

Though it smacked of charades I relayed the message to Bishop. 'How do you want your money?' I asked.

'I don't care, so long as it's in twenties.'

He wouldn't care, would he? If Sir William were right and the money was just a symbol to him.

'Did you hear that, Commissioner?' Pope asked. 'Can you manage it in twenty pound notes?'

'It will be easier that way,' the commissioner said. 'Less to count. We'll send it up.'

Just like that, eh? A million pounds in twenty pound notes and they send it up. Presumably they'd have to scour the banks, or with luck the Bank of England would have it in discarded used notes waiting to be pulped.

'I'm afraid I have to interrupt again,' Sir William said. 'You realize that if you pay this money it'll have to be done in conditions of complete secrecy. Frankly, I can't see you keeping that matter a secret for very long. Once it becomes known by the popular press that such a payment has been made you'll unleash an enormous number of similar kidnap attempts. It won't be possible for Royal Persons to enjoy the freedom they now possess. Everywhere they go they will need to be surrounded by Secret Service men and plain clothes detectives.'

Silence in and out of the office. Silence on the radio link-up. Then suddenly the voice of the commissioner was heard saying 'Did you hear that, Sir?' I realized that other people were on the network which would be using an ultra high frequency that could not be intercepted.

A very familiar voice came on the air. 'Yes, we heard that. We'll need time to think about that.'

Time. There it was again. There just wasn't any time. I had completely accepted Pope's mode of thought. I counted myself among the half that didn't believe Prince Charles was on that yacht, that believed he was lying somewhere imprisoned, suffering a slow death that would take its final curtain in a short time.

The commissioner's voice broke in. 'Concentrate all your efforts, Chief Superintendent Pope, on finding Prince Charles. This line will stay open. You can have all the resources you need. Just ask for them.'

The line to us clicked closed but I knew the extension would remain open while the discussion ranged back and forth over what Sir William had said. It was not a decision I would like to make. It was not a decision that any ordinary person could make. What would I do and say if I had to counter-balance those responsibilities?

I looked at Bishop. 'You know what the decision is going to be,' I said to him. 'They're going to decide not to pay you. You won't get your money. It's not just Prince Charles, it's everybody else. *All* the sons of *all* the people who just happen to have been born in the Royal line. It'll be a very hard decision to make but, from somewhere you and I wouldn't know about, they'll find the strength to make it. Give it up. Tell me the truth; tell me if you know where Prince Charles is and I promise I'll do everything I can to get a new way of life for you. I'll get you the best legal help and the best medical advice. I'll find you somewhere decent to live, start you up in a little business. . . .'

'After the Law has run its course,' Sir William surprised me by saying. 'Mr Bishop must clearly understand that the Law will have to take its course!' I could see his point. I was thinking only of the immediate short-term solution to our problem. Sir William, wisely, was thinking of Bishop's future life which could only have relevance if Bishop accepted his responsibility towards the rest of the community. I wasn't concerned with long-term effects. I was thinking as a father, drawing a parallel between my thoughts of my daughter Helen and the thoughts of any other parents when the life of a loved one is in jeopardy.

Bishop had the cynical look on his face that told me both I and Sir William were wasting our time. 'If you knew how often that sort of thing has been said to me,' he said. 'A golden rosy future if only I'll stop doing what I want to do and start doing what somebody else wants.'

I had a sudden mental picture. Bishop, crouching in his own excrement at the bottom of a hole lined with bamboo; people leaning over the edge guarding their noses from the stink and saying 'if only you'll sign this confession, if only you'll give us this piece of information, we'll bring you out of the hole and give you a bath and you can live comfortably again.' I could see Bishop standing in a line; a man behind a desk littered with yellowing government paper saying, 'I'm trying to do my best for you but the only vacancy we can offer you is . . .' I could see a woman pushing a pen across a piece of paper and saying, with awesome finality, 'if only you were married, if only you had some dependants, then we could give you a supplementary allowance. But we'd need to know where you'd worked for the last five years, and exactly how much you'd earned. . . .'

'I can't trust you,' Bishop said, 'any more than I could trust the rest of them. You're all the same. You've built a life of walls around yourselves and anyone outside is a wild creature from the wilderness. You'll let us come behind your walls, but the cost to get in is more than I'm prepared to pay!' He was becoming agitated; he sat upright in the chair, clutching its arms as if preparing to launch himself. 'I want my million pounds,' he said, and his voice grew loud and shrill.'*I want my million pounds!*'

'He has an idée fixe,' Sir William said. 'It would take extensive and prolonged therapy to get rid of it. He's certainly not prepared to trust you yet.'

Pope had been watching us and didn't seem surprised by Bishop's outburst.

Bishop sprang up from the chair, wild-eyed and staring, his face and his mouth working. Surprisingly his target was not me, not Sir William, but the enormous bulk of Chief Detective Superintendent Pope who was standing now about six feet from Bishop's chair solid on his two feet like a rock. Bishop sprang at him, his hands raised as if to claw, as if the sleeping tiger within him had suddenly been aroused and was after blood. Pope didn't move his body, merely pulled his head back on his shoulders, looking surprised as Bishop pounded ineffectually against his chest and shoulders. Then Pope raised his right hand, clamped it like a cap on the top of Bishop's head and straightened his elbow. Bishop was pushed from him but continued to swing. Sir William was already out of his chair and I had leaped forward, knowing what to expect. It looked as if Pope were measuring Bishop for a left-handed slam that could break Bishop's neck.

'Don't hit him!' Sir William said, 'don't hit him!' his voice pleading. Pope grunted and he kept his left hand down by his side; but he pushed with his right, forward and down, and Bishop spun from under the crushing grip of that right hand and slid backwards, bent at the middle, until the chair came behind his legs and he toppled back into it, gasping for breath and crying.

'We've been too soft with this fellow,' Pope said. 'Now we've got him assaulting a police officer. I'll charge him with that if nothing else.' He walked the two paces forward to the chair. 'Stop that racket,' he said, 'you're a grown man, not a child.'

Bishop shot him a look of pure hatred. I felt scared. Any of us can lose his temper and even a chief superintendent is human.

'*Where is Prince Charles?*' Pope asked, his great bulk poised menacingly in front of Bishop, his hand held as if ready to strike.

Don't let him hit Bishop, I prayed. He'll kill him.

Sir William put out his hand and grasped Pope's shoulder but Pope shrugged him aside, all his venom, all his force, directed at that cowering figure in the chair. 'What time was it when you kidnapped him?' he asked. 'Did you kidnap the detective too? Where were they? In the mews? In the garage? Can you drive a van? Did you have a Bedford van parked there, a Ford Transit perhaps? We can check. Come on, answer me!' His words exploded in Bishop's face, his questions a pounding artillery barrage that thumped the air.

'He won't answer you,' Sir William kept saying, 'he won't!'

'Please, Sir William, leave him to me. Where were you when you kidnapped the prince?' He paused, but our ears were still ringing with the questions, like the brief lull in a tank battle that comes before the final dreadful onslaught. I knew the questions would pound on and on, breaking down resistance, slamming Bishop over and over again, until all he wanted was the peace an answer alone could bring.

'I . . . I . . .' Bishop tried to articulate through the sobs that pulled the air out of his lungs.

'Jock,' Pope shouted without even moving, 'get in here, quick, with a glass of water.'

Jock obeyed immediately though the water was in a cup. Pope took it from him; I thought he was going to fling it in Bishop's face. He thrust it forward so vigorously and with such impatience that some of it slopped out and as Bishop drained the cup Pope beckoned me forward. I knew what to do. It's a technique. Suddenly I realized that despite the cataclysmic display of energy that would have frightened even the hardest person and had certainly scared Sir William and me, he was ice cold and calculating, like a general commanding a battle who lays down a softening barrage and then orders the infantry forward.

I took the cup from Bishop's hands. He had got the shakes. 'Did you get them in the garage?' I asked softly. 'Did you have a Bedford van in the garage? How did you do it, one man against two? Did you have a revolver in the garage with the Bedford van? Pointed the revolver at them, told them to get into the back of the van? Was that how it happened?' I paused. 'You're going to have to tell us in the long run. Come on, make it now. Was it in the garage?'

He shook his head.

That was an answer of a sort. The first one we'd got. Pope saw it and leaned further forward. 'Where then, in the mews?'

Bishop shook his head again.

'In the street?' I said. 'The hallway of Lord Popham's building? Your company has the contract to clean that building. You were in the hallway sweeping the steps, were you?'

Sir William had come round the side of the chair and he reached his hand forward and touched Bishop's wrist. I saw Bishop flinch. Sir William glanced at the slim watch he was wearing, no doubt metering Bishop's pulse.

Pope's savagery had caused the adrenalin to flow and the sobs had stopped. Bishop's breathing was returning to normal. Now he'd be able to speak again, to answer our questions.

When Pope spoke again his voice was soft, so that one could hardly hear the question. That also was part of the technique. It's amazing how many people ask 'What did you say?' and then, when the question is asked again, answer it without thought. Bishop fell into it.

'What did you say?' he asked.

When Pope spoke his voice had gone up only a notch but he'd secured Bishop's attention. 'Just tell us in your own words how you managed to pull off the kidnapping. It's quite an achievement to take two men, one of them a detective, and we'd like to know how you did it.' Bishop opened his mouth to speak. I stopped breathing. Now we were going to get it. Now this farcical charade would end.

'You can ask me questions till you're blue in the face but I'm not going to answer,' Bishop said.

Air escaped from Pope like a burst tyre. Moving surprisingly quickly for such an enormous man his hand reached in and grasped Bishop's shoulder. Sir William brought his hand across and grabbed Pope's wrist but I knew he wasn't checking his pulse. Pope shook Bishop slowly but with a bone-cracking power. 'You'll answer my questions,' he growled, 'even if I have to take you apart.'

Beneath the network of the crossed arms of Sir William and Pope, Bishop's hands were busy; in a quick flurry he threw open his jacket and his shirt again and revealed the macabre sight I had already seen of his chest lacerated with scars of old wounds, the flesh bunched and withered in scabby tissue, browns and purples and the albino white where skin had been peeled away and had grown again. It was a sickening sight.

'I've been questioned in ways you wouldn't dream possible,' he said. 'There's hardly a bone in my body that hasn't at some time been broken.'

Pope drew away and Sir William's hand dropped to his side.

'Good God man,' Sir William said, 'good God!'

Of the four of us, only he had the medical knowledge to understand the enormity of what had been done to this suffering husk of a man. Quite unconsciously he put out his hand and touched the scar tissue on Bishop's chest where the nipple on his breast should have been but no longer was. He looked at Pope with anguish in his eyes. 'In the name of God, man . . .' he said.

Pope, too, was visibly shaken. He stood upright and looked at Bishop's chest, then he looked at Sir William. 'I didn't know,' he said, 'I didn't realize. I couldn't have realized.'

Sir William drew Bishop's shirt back across his chest and buttoned it. He closed Bishop's coat. Pope walked back to his desk and stood there looking down. He walked across to the door that connected us with the next room. 'Can you get me some coffee, Jock?' he asked, 'strong and black.' He turned round. 'Would anybody else like anything? How about you, Mr Bishop?'

Bishop shook his head. 'Now can I have my million pounds?' he said, his voice quiet and even as if his request were a perfectly ordinary normal simple one.

Pope took in a lungful of air and expelled it in a despairing sigh. What can we do with such a man, his look seemed to say.

'There's the idée fixe again,' Sir William reminded us.

Silence had settled on the room like a blanket of death. Pope took his coffee but drank only a third of it before pushing the cup away. He sat back at his desk, his head in his hands. Then he seemed to rally his scattered forces.

'What we have,' he said, deliberately ponderous to command our attention, 'is a matter of detection. Don't let's try any more appeals to Mr Bishop's "reason" because I don't think that, after what has been done to him, we have any right to expect him to have any. Let's concentrate all our thinking on the few facts we do have, and then speculate a little. For the moment I want to forget about the grey suit, the green tie, the yacht being moored at Chatham and not at Cowes. I want to concentrate on the part of Bishop's ultimatum that says, "if I don't get what I want, Prince Charles will die in, or within, eight hours." That gives us a six o'clock deadline. Now, does he mean "in", or "within"?'

' "In",' I said.

'You're sure about that?'

'Absolutely. He started off by saying "within", but when I pressed him, he changed it to "in" and that's how it's stayed.'

'You realize the difference, of course. In method. Let's say you administered a killing poison to someone. That someone could be said to be dying from the moment you gave them the poison. Unless you returned "within", shall we say, eight hours, that person would be dead of that poison. But as long as you got back in time to administer the antidote, they would stay alive. On the other hand, you tie somebody, set them in a cellar next to a bomb which has a timed detonation. Set for eight hours. In other words, at six o'clock the detonator will fire, the bomb will explode. At six o'clock. The person will die "in" eight hours.'

'I'm certain it was "in".'

'Right. Let's think about method. About possible methods. Any thoughts, Sir William?'

'I don't like the "poison and antidote" technique. It implies a lot of knowledge I don't think Mr Bishop possesses. It also implies a source, and such things are not left lying about.'

'Bishop worked for a Cleaning Company and they have access to many places,' I said. 'They could have contracts for a hospital with access to the Dispensary. Contracts for a chemists' wholeseller's warehouse. Chemists' shops. Bishop has a room full of books. One of them could be a medical book on poisons.'

Pope shouted down the line. 'Jock, I want someone to go to Bishop's place in Arlington Villas and skim quickly through the titles of his books. Bring back any that have to do with medical subjects. In particular, poisons.'

'Right, Chief.'

'I also want somebody to see the Sparkling Cleaning Company, and telephone a list of every job that Bishop has ever worked on. Better still, I want a list of any contracts they may have, whether Bishop has worked on them or not, with chemists' shops, hospitals, pharmaceutical wholesellers – anywhere, in fact, where a supply of drugs is kept.'

'Right, Chief.'

'Bishop might have paid a call on a fellow employee working in such a place,' he said to us.

Sir William was shaking his head. 'I don't think so,' he said, 'but you're right not to take a chance.'

'I think that's all we can do on the poisons idea,' Pope said, 'unless either of you has anything else to offer?'

'Lots of people save medicines,' Bishop said, to no one in particular, almost as if he were talking to himself. 'Mrs Calleja has a cupboard full.'

'Jock,' Pope shouted, 'while he's there, the chap searching Bishop's room can look for poisons, anything out of the ordinary.'

'A bottle of aspirins would kill a man, if his stomach wasn't pumped out in time,' Bishop said.

Pope turned on him, was about to say something but with great effort restrained himself. 'What do you think about the aspirin method, Sir William?' he asked.

Sir William had been thinking. 'Possible,' he said, 'but not likely. In fact, I don't like any of this chemical business. The basic problem is that all chemicals behave differently inside different people. What will affect one man will have no effect whatsoever on another. The body's own chemistry plays a large part in that. It would be very very difficult to find any chemical you could administer to a man and then guarantee a certain effect "within" or "in" a certain time. It depends so very much on what chemicals have preceded the one you administer, and Mr Bishop couldn't know that, could he? You can administer some chemicals that would kill an average man, but the patient may already have developed an immunity from previous dosage. I just don't like this chemical approach, unless it's combined with some sort of timing device. A phial of prussic acid, shall we say, that will be broken open at a certain time. But that's a very complicated, very Heath Robinson sort of business.'

'Remember the books, Sir William,' I said. 'Bishop may be a fan of Edgar Wallace, Edgar Allan Poe, Sherlock Holmes. That's the sort of method mystery writers used to love to write about. And those writers did very accurate research. Most of their methods were ingenious but accurate. I remember one about an arrow fired by an apparatus that retracted itself when a key was turned. It worked.'

I didn't waste time telling them that, as a young man, I was fascinated by the criminology of people like Sherlock Holmes and spent hours working out the crimes in their books. I'd tried the arrow trick myself. It worked so well the arrow fired and stuck in my shoulder. I still carry the scar. Bishop, I thought, was the sort of man to be fascinated by those problems. But we didn't have time to sift the collected works of Poe, Wallace, and Conan Doyle.

'I still don't like it,' Sir William said. 'It implies a collection of too many separate acts, all requiring thought, planning and technique. Plus coordination. I'd prefer to look for something spontaneous. Something that could happen on impulse, almost without planning. I don't think Mr Bishop, if he will forgive me saying so, is a man to bother with much planning. I think he's more a man to be moved by emotional impulses.'

' "Prince Charles will die in eight hours", that's our key statement,' Pope said. 'Bishop is certain of that, I take it?'

Both Sir William and I nodded. What little we'd heard from Bishop so far was quite positive about that aspect of the kidnapping. In several senses, the kidnapping was different from others. Usually the kidnapper takes his victim, hides with him somewhere, and communicates with the relatives by a variety of methods that don't reveal either the kidnapper's identity or his victim's location. Bishop walking in to the station was different. Come to think of it, if his request for money succeeded, it was the most simple and elementary thing to do. So much easier than a message telling us to leave the money in a parcel by the third tree in the Park.

'One thought occurs to me immediately,' I said. 'If we accept the point made both by Dr Gervis and Sir William that Bishop is a loner, then he would have to leave the prince and his detective somewhere absolutely safe. Somewhere they couldn't escape from. Either they are conscious, or under sedation. Thinking about the chemical business, again if Sir William is right, we can discount that they might be sedated. Simply because Bishop wouldn't trust the effectiveness of the sedative.'

'You have a good point there,' Pope said. 'Lack of trust of people would rule out an accomplice. Lack of trust of things would rule out a sedative or any form of time mechanism, wouldn't it? If he's here, and there's nothing to prevent us keeping him here, how can he be positive the death is going to be achieved in eight hours?'

'It's only three hours now,' I reminded him.

'In three hours, then? If he doesn't trust any*thing* or any*body*, how's he going to do it? Starvation – well, nobody dies in eight hours of starvation. Thirst?' He shook his head at that one. 'It would be easy to take two people somewhere under a gun, tie them up, plant a timed bomb beside them.'

'That lack of trust surely would extend even further,' I said. 'He wouldn't even trust the knots if he tied them up. . . .'

'All right, a chain, with a lock. . . .'

'Locks can be picked, chains can be sawn through. . . . No, Chief Superintendent, if we continue this line of thinking about him not trusting anything or anybody, we rule out the employment of any extra device whatsoever. . . .'

The voice of Jock came through the open door. 'I've got Pearson on the line, Chief. He's been to look at the books.'

'Put him on One.'

'He's on.'

'You've been quick, Pearson. Well done lad! What can you tell us?'

The voice of Pearson came over the loudspeaker harsh and metallic, no doubt the distortion of the walkie talkie into which he was speaking, amplified by the network of lines down to which it passed to reach us. 'Well, first of all Sir, about the medicines. There's absolutely nothing in the basement room that you could call a medicine unless you count toothpaste in the sink. No aspirins, no sleeping-pills, nothing. . . .'

He had taught himself to survive, hadn't he, in the prison camp. There'd be a lot of the Stoic in him. If he had a headache he'd be the sort of man to take a walk or deep breathing exercises rather than a pill. I can understand that; I'm a bit that way myself.

'Now about the books, Sir,' the constable said. 'He's got a lot. You understand I could only skim along the rows. I didn't see anything you might call a medical book. Mostly they were science fiction and war books. Crikey, he seems to have every war book that's ever been written.'

Sir William was nodding, and I could see the sort of perverse logic that would make a man who had suffered as Bishop had read about the war, about wars in general, seeking possibly subconsciously to discover the reason why.

'Any detective thrillers?' I asked loudly, knowing the microphone would pick up my voice. 'Conan Doyle, Edgar Allen Poe,

The Adventures of Fu Manchu, anything like that?'

The constable thought for a moment. 'Nooo . . .' he said slowly. 'I don't remember nothing like that. Like I said, it was mostly science fiction and war books.' I heard him chuckle. 'One shelf of books struck me as a bit odd.'

'What was that?' Pope barked.

'Romantic fiction. You know, Ethel M. Dell. Sort of stuff my wife reads. A whole pile of the magazines, too. *Woman's Own, Woman, Woman's Realm.* Looks as if he had a woman living down there, but I took a quick look round and could find no trace of hairs in the bathroom, no woman's clothes about.'

'He needn't pursue that line of investigation,' Sir William said quietly. 'Many men starved of affection read romantic fiction. For many it's their only image of love.'

'You've done a good job, Constable,' the chief superintendent said. 'Stand by in case we need anything else.'

'Could I ask one more question,' I said, then pitched my voice a little louder. 'Can you remember, Constable, if there were any gadgets about the place? Anything to suggest the man who occupied the room might be a handyman? In particular any clock parts or electrical things?'

While I had been talking Jock had come to the doorway and beckoned to the chief superintendent, who walked across. 'Where do you want it?' I heard him whisper. 'In a cell?'

'No, in here.'

Jock looked surprised but nodded.

Again the voice of the constable was hesitant as he searched his memory. 'Nooo . . .' he said again. 'I can't remember nothing like that. No hobby things of any kind. I can't remember seeing any tools.'

'Bishop wouldn't have the patience,' Sir William said quietly. 'If he started a hobby he'd never finish. The place would be littered with things he'd taken up and then abandoned.'

When the line closed down we heard Jock's voice again. 'I have the other constable on the line ringing from Sparkling Cleaning. Shall I put him on?'

'Yes,' Pope said.

'This is Constable Watkins reporting from Sparkling Cleaning Company of 5, Lisson Crescent, Paddington, West 2, relating to the inquiry that's been set in train . . .'

'We know all that,' Pope barked. 'Have they any contracts along the lines outlined to you?'

'I've examined the relevant files and information. . . .'

Pope looked up at the ceiling. Some men just can't speak out straight but Pope was too old a hand to try a second push. We all listened while the constable rambled on. Sparkling Cleaning Company had no contract of any kind with any company that dealt in pharmaceuticals. They did not clean any chemists' shops, hospitals, dispensaries, pharmaceutical wholesellers or stockists. No factories where drugs were manufactured. While the constable's voice rambled on Pope got up and walked to the doorway.

'Have a word with him when he's finished Jock,' the chief superintendent said.

'He's from Traffic,' Jock explained. 'He was the nearest man.'

Pope nodded and sat down at his desk again. 'All this seems to be heading one way,' he said. 'No medicines, no hobbies, no timed explosion. It adds up. But where the hell does it lead us?'

We were all thinking as hard as we could. I think the idea came to both Pope and me simultaneously.

'What time is high tide, Jock?' Pope shouted. I had just been about to say 'natural phenomena' but of course of the natural phenomena the only one with a time factor is the tide. The tide went out at a certain time each day and exposed places a man could reach, mudflats, beaches, quarries, underground caves; then the tide came back in and covered those places again, with swirling black water that would drown any man who could not flee. Bishop's eyes were on Sir William and in them I saw defiance.

The voice of Jock came back. 'It varies you know, Chief Superintendent, up and down the river.'

'Give me an average time for Westminster.'

I knew what the tide was going to be even before Jock said it. 'Six o'clock!' Two hours and forty-five minutes from now. High tide.

Pope pressed the switch on his microphone. 'Commissioner,' he said, 'we're going to need a lot of help in a hurry. But first we require some information.'

'We're standing by,' the commissioner's voice said.

'Thinking about the tide, Commissioner, and about places where you could put two men, where they would drown when the tide came up. Preferably somewhere you wouldn't need to tie them.'

'Could they be held unconscious?'

'By drugs? We don't think so.'

'That eliminates a boat wreck lying on the mudflat?'

'Yes, it does.'

'Or any kind of container. You understand, Chief Superintendent, I'm just thinking out loud.'

'It would have to be some kind of underground cellar wouldn't it, or a natural cave.' I voiced my thoughts and the chief superintendent nodded agreement.

The commissioner heard what I said. 'That's a job for the Ministry of Public Works,' he said.

'You might also get on to the London office of *National Geographic Magazine* and the secretary of the London branch of the British Speleological Society.'

'And the Sub Aqua Club,' the chief superintendent added.

'I can follow your line of thinking,' the commissioner said. 'Leave it with me.'

All along the bank of the Thames the tides flow in, the tides flow out, as far as, was it Teddington, was Teddington the limit of the tidal part of the Thames?

'It'll have to be somewhere fairly close,' I said. 'We don't know the exact time factor but assuming he took them, shall we say, at seven o'clock, he was in here by ten, so that only gives him three hours. In that time he's got to drive them somewhere, dump them, secure them, and get back here.' Even as I spoke I realized that still left a hell of a lot of the Thames with both banks equally likely.

Pope stretched himself, relaxing for a few moments. He stood up, pensive, walked across to where Bishop was sitting, He reached his hand down but didn't touch Bishop. 'You had a bad time, lad, I know that. What's been done to you I wouldn't want to see done to any man. Somehow you've got yourself on the wrong track. I wish I had the wisdom and the time to help Sir William here get you back on the right track again.'

'It's no good. . . .' Bishop said.

'I know it's no good, lad. I'm not trying to have a go at you. But I'm a police officer and it's up to me to do what I can to prevent this awful thing you just might have done. Let's face it, Prince Charles is a human being and so is that detective. They have rights too, you know. They have problems. We all have problems.' He looked up at me. 'Ring your wife at the hospital, Inspector,' he said. 'Find out how that daughter of yours is.'

Though I resented him using my personal situation I had to admire his technique. I went over to the doorway. 'Could you get me a call to St Matthew's Hospital, Jock,' I said, 'but put it on a telephone.'

'Number two,' he said, 'on the chief super's desk.'

I could hear the chief superintendent's voice going on, calm and in tones that normally would have been persuasive.

'A terrible thing has happened to Inspector Armstrong's daughter,' he said to Bishop. 'She suffered an appendix that burst. They had to operate on her in the ambulance. Now the poor innocent kid has peritonitis and she's in the Intensive Care Unit. Inspector Armstrong would be over there if we didn't need him here.'

They found Sarah for me and put her on the telephone. 'There's no change, love,' she said, 'or I would have rung. It's taking such a long time. That nice young doctor's been out but I'm very worried. I don't suppose there's any chance of you coming over here?'

I felt like a heel. 'I'm afraid there isn't, love, not just yet.' I sensed rather than heard the slight break in her voice.

'It's just, oh, I know there's nothing you could do or anything, but it would be nice to have your hand to hold. You're always so confident. You give me such strength. Anyway, you've got your job to do. If you were down the mine you couldn't come rushing over. What is the job, anyway? Something big . . .?'

'I can't tell you, love, and I'm afraid I can't stay. I'll keep in touch with you as and when I can.' I lowered my voice. 'My thoughts are with you all the time,' I said. 'Ring me, won't you, promise you'll ring me if there's any news. I can always take a telephone call.'

'No change, eh?' Chief Superintendent Pope said when I put

the telephone down. The bastard had been listening. 'If only Mr Bishop would let you get over there....'

'*You* could let him,' Bishop said, speaking directly to the chief superintendent. 'Give me my million pounds and send me on my way and the inspector could be in St Matthew's in ten minutes. I went there for ten years, to the Out-Patients Department. They wanted to tear off my skin and start again.'

The money arrived.

The door opened and two uniformed sergeants carried it in, with an inspector to guide them. 'Put it down there,' he said, fussily. The money was in two suitcases, canvas with a tartan pattern on them, the ones you can fold up when they're empty. These were obviously full.

'Who's going to sign for them?' the inspector said.

I looked at the chief superintendent, then reached for the pad. It's not every day you get to put your signature beneath the figure £1,000,000. The two sergeants put the suitcases on the floor; each had a chain round the centre of his suitcase, attached to a handcuff around his wrist. I signed the piece of paper, feeling like Burton. Then the inspector produced a key from his trouser pocket, attached to a chain and a key-ring, with a leather thong that fitted round a button. It seemed a slender way to safeguard a million pounds. He took the leather thong off his trouser button and handed the whole thing to me. I don't have buttons on my trousers. I used the key to unlock the handcuffs and separate the sergeants from their responsibilities. Both sprang upright. I think they were sorry to see the money go, as if they hadn't lost hope until that moment that some of it might stick to them. The cases were not locked. No point. Anyone could slit open that canvas with a sharp nail-file.

One million pounds in twenties. Fifty thousand twenty pound notes. It seemed to be burning a hole in the carpet. I hefted one of the bags. I wouldn't like to carry it very far. He wouldn't need to, would he? He could afford to buy a taxi.

The voice of the commissioner came on the loudspeaker. 'You should have just received the money,' it said. It sounded ghostly, 1984-ish.

Pope answered him. 'Yes, we have it.'

I put one of the suitcases flat on Pope's desk, beside the

microphone. 'Shall we take a look inside?' I said.

'Come over here, Mr Bishop,' Pope said.

Bishop walked across the carpet showing neither eagerness nor pleasure. He could have been coming to look at a photograph. Sir William came over, too, an apologetic look on his face.

'We're all attracted by the sight of actual money,' he said, by way of an excuse.

Slowly I pulled the zipper round the outside of the case, waiting until I had taken it all the way before attempting to lift the top. Slowly, conscious of the drama of the moment, I pulled the top back. Inside was a sheet of brown paper. I lifted the brown paper and set it aside. The money was in neat stacks. Some notes were brand new, others had been used. All were bound into bundles by bank papers endorsed with the names and signs of several of the Big Five. Pope reached in his hand and drew out one of the five by five, twenty-five stacks. The notes were bundled in hundreds. There were ten bundles in the stack. Pope counted them as he put them back, one by one, so that Bishop could see him. Then he counted the numbers of stacks out loud, touching each one as he did so. When he had finished, he placed the brown paper back on the top.

'Zip it up and let's have the other one,' he said.

I zipped it, put that case on the floor and replaced it with the other. It was filled in exactly the same way. I put back the brown paper and zipped that bag up too, regretting seeing the money go out of my sight.

Pope sat at his desk. His hands were on the desk where the money had been. With the microphone to one side, he could have been Richard Baker, ready to read the nine o'clock news. 'I can see something is troubling you, Sir William,' he said. 'You don't like that money being here, do you?'

We were all sitting down as if waiting for the next act of some ghastly play-reading, where drama would suddenly take on real dimensions and fiction became fact.

'I question the wisdom of bringing it into this room and showing it to Mr Bishop. Up to now, the money has been a symbol, not a reality. It's much easier to let go of a symbol. Any resolve he might have can only be hardened by the sight of the money. Now that he's actually *seen* it, he'll want to possess it. It will be harder to get him to cooperate with you, since he's seen what he will lose if he does so. I didn't realize you were going to bring the money in here. I thought it would be kept outside somewhere and only produced when necessary.'

His thinking ran parallel to mine. Without benefit of psychiatric training and insight, I could only think the actual sight of the money could have a bad affect.

'We take a chance by showing Bishop that money,' Pope said, 'but we also convince him we are sincere. Sincere not only about the money, but about everything else we say. We *show* him one million pounds, the sum he asked for. We make him realize the enormity of his request. We bring him down to earth, if you like to think of it that way. I'm not going to give you that money, Mr Bishop, until half past five. And I'm only going to give it to you then if I have failed. I don't think I am going to fail. You could say I'm gambling with you, and that money is *my* stake in the game. Your continued liberty is *your* stake. You see, I believe that without any cooperation from you, I can beat you by the process of detection. You may think we know nothing, that we shall continue to know nothing so long as you hold your tongue. But we can find out everything we want to know about you by the normal process of detection. Believe me, Bishop, when this case is over and I've bested you, I'm going to make certain every criminal in the country who bothers to read the papers, listens to the radio or watches television, will know how we did it. It'll make a fascinating story, and your refusal to give us any help will make the story valid. It'll be the greatest single piece of crime prevention we've ever done in this country. We're going to succeed Bishop, Inspector Armstrong, Sir William, and I, because behind us we have the finest police machine that has ever been put together. You can sit there, Bishop, you can watch and listen and look at two suitcases containing a million pounds and without tricks, without your cooperation we'll beat you.

'Jock,' he said, raising his voice just sufficient to let it be heard in the next room, 'get the team from Police Public Relations. Stills man, sixteen-millimetre movie man, the lot. And get me a man who can write a story, because we're going to give him one today that'll make criminological history.'

Sir William was agitated, that was plain to see. So was I, but in a different way. The chief superintendent was putting a lot of faith in us. A lot beside that money was at stake, including the life of Prince Charles and a detective.

The commissioner's voice came on the loudspeaker. 'I heard that, Arthur, and frankly, I wish you luck. I've been told, however, that at half past five that money must be paid over and the man allowed to go away without surveillance. Understood?'

'Understood, Commissioner,' Pope said.

'Now I have some information for you. We've put together a list of the places you were asking about. We've taken as our guide lines somewhere a man could get into at low tide, but couldn't get out of at high tide, without special apparatus like diving gear and so forth. Somewhere that's accessible by road, and somewhere you could get to and not be seen. For example, there's a place beneath the Palace of Westminster, but you'd have to get there from a boat. I presume a boat is out of the question?'

Pope looked for my opinion. 'Yes, I think the time factor rules out a boat. Near the Palace of Westminster.'

Pope agreed.

'Then we're left with three places. We already have teams standing by. One is down by Blackfriars. There's a yard into which you could drive. It's not used now. You go down some steps to the riverside. In there is a brick-lined construction that used to be cellar. You can get into it. The river police know about it and have wired it off time and time again, but the kids always mess about with the wire. We're searching that place now, but you understand we have to send divers down. The Sub-Aqua Club is helping and we're waiting for a man to arrive. The second one is at Mortlake. It used to be a brewery. Again, a brick construction, at the bottom of a lane. You could get there without being seen. You have to go under an archway. We've talked to a man there; the archway is covered by nine o'clock these mornings. . . .'

Neither of those places sounded right to me. They'd ignored the essential part of the operation. I held up my hand, feeling like a schoolboy.

'Hang on a minute, Commissioner,' Pope said, 'Inspector Armstrong wants to say something,'

'Imagine the scene when they get there,' I said. 'Bishop has a gun. He's put them into the van, taken them out at the far end. "Right, walk," he says. They walk forward, down to this archway. They walk under the archway, through waist-high water. Once they're through, he says, "stay there". Then he drives away. What's to prevent them ducking back out?'

'Possibly he knocks them out before he leaves . . .?'

I was shaking my head. 'He wouldn't rely on that, would he? Hit them with a gun, and they could recover consciousness at any time. Say five minutes after he left. Still time to dive down below the archway and get out again.'

'I see what you mean,' the commissioner said over the loudspeaker. 'We'll have to think again.'

'It has to be somewhere a man could get into, but couldn't get out again without help.'

'Leave it with us,' the commissioner said. 'We've assembled enough experts, all on the end of telephones.'

'We're still trying to trace that yacht,' Pope said, 'but with the existing weather conditions we don't stand much of a chance. Apparently the mist has come down, and visibility in that area is no more than twenty-five feet.'

I was suddenly struck by the knowledge that I had been the one to inspire all this activity. My God, would I look a fool if it turned out that Prince Charles was on the yacht after all with his detective, sitting out a misty passage, half of him cursing because they couldn't sail, the other half welcoming a day of true isolation, away from the cares and responsibilities of being Heir to the Throne.

Pope walked next door to confer with Jock.

I sat on the arm of Bishop's chair. Of the four of us he alone seemed completely relaxed. Sir William was still disturbed by the presence of that money and the effect it would have on Bishop's determination.

'What do you intend to do with the money if you get it?' I asked.

Bishop smiled at me. 'Buy a new way of life for myself,' he said, 'a life where I don't have to answer to anybody in order to get enough to live.'

'A car; a yacht; a pad in the Mediterranean sun? The West Indies?'

'If you're trying to find out where I might be . . .?'

'No, I wasn't being a policeman at that moment. I was just curious as to what you'd do. A million is a lot of money. You will be able to live handsomely off the interest. That is, if you're ever able to put in into a bank.'

'I imagine that could be done. Bit by bit,' Sir William said. 'You'd have to deposit it in small amounts, change it in small amounts in a bureau de change. . . .'

'Not me,' Bishop said, 'I'll keep the money with me. As money. Change it only when I need to.'

'Of course, that's right, you wouldn't trust a bank, would you?' Bishop would be a strictly cash-under-the-mattress type.

The door opened and Chief Inspector Roberts came in. He motioned to me with his hand to tell me to ignore him if I were occupied. He went into the other room to talk with Chief Superintendent Pope. I was pleased he hadn't disturbed us; although I hoped Bishop would think we were just chatting, I did have an objective.

'At least with all that money you won't be short of friends,' I said. 'Not like Arlington Villas. Life must have been very lonely in Arlington Villas, with only Mrs Calleja to talk to.'

'You don't *talk* to Mrs Calleja,' he said, 'you listen. She does all the talking.'

'So she's not nosey? Doesn't ask questions about your private life. That's good. Too many people are nosey. Like that man you were telling us about. . . .'

'Oh him, living in the past off his memories. And always questions. What mob were you in, and then a twenty minute story about what *he* did in the war. Then, where do you live? All that.'

'He must have been coming to take his lunch with you for quite a while before you decided you couldn't stand it any more.'

He looked a bit sheepish. 'Yes, I stuck him for as long as I could.'

'It was a pity you couldn't find a friend. Somebody you

could talk to. Come to think of it, you do have a friend, don't you. According to Mrs Calleja . . .'

He was instantly suspicious. 'Mrs Calleja? What does she know?'

'You remember, she told our man you used to go away for a couple of nights occasionally, to stay with your girlfriend.'

'What girlfriend? I don't have a girlfriend.'

'Oh, I'm sorry, I must have misunderstood! It's a pity you don't have a girlfriend. Someone to talk to. I get home at nights sometimes and am I relieved to find my wife at home, waiting for me. Just to talk to about things other than police work. It's a marvellous change, I can tell you. Just to have somebody to talk to.'

'We all need that,' Sir William said. 'Otherwise we'd go completely out of our minds.'

'I'm not mad, if that's what you're getting at. I'm not out of my mind. I have people to talk to, if I want to. Anytime I want, I can go and find people to talk to.'

'And then, when you've had enough, you can go back to Arlington Villas, eh? You can get bored with people, sometimes.'

'You can't rely on them, that's the trouble. You can't trust them. You may think you're getting along fine with somebody, but then they pop out a question, something that has nothing to do with them. Of course, young people are all the same.'

'Young people and old people. Mrs Calleja's an old person.'

'Young people are worse than old ones.'

'And boys are worse than girls . . .?'

'They certainly are,' he said.

My mind was racing, but I didn't dare even glance in Sir William's direction. So, Bishop used to pop off now and then. Stay away for a while, come back. Young people ask embarrassing questions. Was I right in thinking that Bishop had a friend, a young friend, tucked away somewhere? Someone he could go and see, someone he could talk to, until that young person, no doubt in all innocence, asked an embarrassing question, not meaning any harm. 'What did you do with your hands, Jim? Where did you get that scar on your neck? Why aren't you married?' There'd be a million questions, innocently asked, that could sever the tender link between an older man and a young boy. I didn't feel there would be any homosexuality in the relationship. For Bishop, the young boy would be somebody to talk to. But here was the difficult part. Bishop used to stay away 'overnight'. That would be difficult, wouldn't it? Young boys are not normally permitted out overnight. Parents want them back home and in bed by dark. Young boys don't live without parents, do they? So, it would seem the 'young boy' must be at least over the age of fifteen. Enough of them about, confused young lads who've run away from parental supervision. Doing 'their thing'. Searching for an identity. Or so they say. For my money, they were escaping the tedious routine of learning how to fit into an adult world.

'Young people can be very difficult to get on with sometimes,' I said. 'They have no respect.'

Bingo, I'd hit it. 'You're damned right,' he said, 'no respect at all. They forget that older people have been through a lot, seen a lot more life than they have. I have a friend called Peter who's just the same . . .' He realized what he'd said and stopped.

'They're all the same. All the same,' I said hurriedly to breach the gap. *'Peter'*, a *'young friend'*. I'd become increasingly unhappy about the way we'd been tackling this 'problem in detection' as Chief Superintendent Pope had so flamboyantly called it. I felt unhappy at the thought of the giant machine that was poised, its wheels geared to mesh and turn every time Pope shouted to Jock, or pressed the switch on his microphone. I agreed with Pope we needed detective work, but disagreed on the method. We needed a calm stillness into which we could drop little pebbles, so that we could see where the ripples went. Bishop was not unapproachable. No man would be, as deprived of human contact as he had been. Of course, the contacts would have to conform to his rules. No aggressive intrusion, no point-blank questions about his life, his way of living. And above all, no subjective value judgements, no forcing him to think along conventional lines of sophisticated conduct. He had a morality, that was obvious, but he had none of the overt observances with which we enslave our lives. He was wearing no tie, for instance. With him, that would not be a conscious act of either rebellion or modernity. He just simply didn't want to be bothered with a tie. This 'young friend', who could he be? More importantly, was the young friend acting with Bishop in the kidnapping? Because if he were, that would change things. That would mean, for example, that provided Bishop could trust his friend, possibly the only person he could trust, then the prince and the detective could have been tied up in a van parked anywhere. The young friend could be guarding them with orders to shoot at a certain time if Bishop didn't return. That could destroy all concepts of 'timed mechanical devices'. It would also put paid to my idea about 'natural phenomena.'

Out of the corner of my eye I saw Pope beckon to me. I got up slowly, stretched, and then walked casually from the room.

CHAPTER SEVEN

'I asked the chief inspector to try to get hold of this man Jackson,' Pope said, 'but apparently he hasn't shown up for work today. He's had a bit of a cold recently, so they think he's tucked up in bed with it.'

'Has someone gone to the house?'

'We don't know where he lives. Apparently he's just moved, and the forwarding address his old landlady gave us was wrong.'

'*Landlady* . . . ?'

'Yes. I thought about that one, too. Apparently Jackson too is a bit of a loner. Not married. No known friends. Apparently he's a very ugly man, not at all prepossessing to look at.'

'His landlady said no girl would look twice at him,' the chief inspector said.

'How old is he?' I asked. 'Could he be described as a "young man"?'

'Hardly. He's turned fifty.'

'Mrs Calleja said he used to visit Bishop sometimes. That's unusual, isn't it? Labour Exchange people don't usually get involved in outside casework, do they?'

'What are you suggesting, Armstrong?' Pope asked. 'That Bishop and Jackson might have been connected?'

I thought about that. Then dismissed the idea. 'Jackson is a lonely man. Bishop comes in several times. They get to know each other across the counter. Jackson decides to take a personal interest, because he is lonely and could do with somebody to talk to, play chess with, that sort of thing. He goes to Bishop's place one day, when Bishop is absent from his job. Tries to persuade Bishop to go back to work. Bishop wouldn't trust a man like that, wouldn't respond to Jackson's overtures of friendship. That's the way I see it, anyway.'

'A typical Inspector Armstrong piece of reasoning,' the chief inspector said. 'Give you one fact, and you'll make the Gospel according to Saint Bill out of it.'

I was miffed. 'I haven't always been wrong, Chief Inspector,

I said. 'Remember the Royal Hall!'

'And you haven't always been right. Remember the time you had us up all night because you "reasoned" that Crombey would only do supermarkets and we staked out the only one in the area, while Crombey was tunnelling his way into a jeweller's shop?'

'We all make mistakes,' I said stiffly.

'Yes, Inspector, but you more often than most, it sometimes seems to me. . . .'

He could have waited until we were alone together before he said that. He didn't have to put me down in front of the chief superintendent. I could see Pope had taken in what had been said, was looking quizzically at me. 'If we're on another of your wild goose chases . . .' he said. Dammit, he was the man who'd been talking about gambling with a million pounds as stake, about beating Bishop with a piece of detection, about calling in the P.R. department. Where were they, by the way? They should have been here by now, taking photographs of God behind his desk, the poor victim in his chair, the hard-working lower orders sitting beside him. Dammit, he didn't need a writer; I could do the script myself. 'With the aid of my excellent force of officers, and remembering that no police effort can succeed without team work, I have been able to prove to this man that crime, at least not in my patch, does NOT pay. . . .'

'If you've involved me with another of your hare-brained schemes, Inspector Armstrong. . . .' Pope said.

The thought was appalling. All those men deployed, all those communications, the entire police force of England available at our command. Royal Personages worried. Buckingham Palace put on a state of alert. And all because a man guessed correctly the colour of another man's tie.

And then the picture hit me. Of course, Sparkling Cleaning Company had the contract to clean Lord Popham's apartment building. Staircases, hallways, windows. Bishop had been working there, pushing a broom. Prince Charles and his detective were going sailing, leaving before the cleaners had a chance to finish. 'Excuse me,' Prince Charles would say as he crossed the wet hallway. Bishop would be surprised to see a royal prince at that hour of the morning. He'd notice the grey lounge suit, the green tie with its coloured stripe. The prince and the detective would doubtless be chatting. 'Hope the weather's good at Chatham.' 'We should have a good day's sailing.' 'Does Lord Wentworth's yacht carry a spinnaker, Sir?' 'Good to get away for a day, out in the Thames where nobody knows.' 'Can I give the Palace a forwarding telephone number, Sir?' 'I'm afraid not, Lord Wentworth tells me his radiophone isn't working. He's had it taken into Decca for repairs. So much the better, no one will be able to get hold of us, to disturb us.' 'What about an emergency, Sir?' 'They can always send out the coastguard if it's something really urgent. . . .'

There were endless possibilities of dialogue Bishop could have overheard to cause him to put two and two together. The prince and his detective would be out of touch all day. What about a kidnap plot? Go into the nearest police station, take a chance, possibly get a million pounds out of it. A crackpot idea, but then, Bishop couldn't be completely sane, could he? I did not doubt that a long-term analysis by Sir William would reveal a vein of insanity. What did Bishop have to lose? If we didn't believe him, we'd throw him out. Possibly charge him with causing a nuisance or some such trivial offence. But if we *did* believe him, perhaps, only perhaps, we might come up with a million. It was a chance a crackpot like Bishop would think worth taking.

Hang on! Was I doing what the chief inspector had just accused me of? Taking a fact and from it, constructing the Gospel according to Saint Bill? I think if the chief hadn't said that, I would have spoken my thoughts out loud to Pope, risking his wrath as the case crumbled about his ears. But I hadn't the guts to say it. 'We can't be certain of anything on a case like this,' I said, aware that I was mumbling. 'We had to take a chance. If there's any possibility that Prince Charles had been kidnapped, any remote possibility . . .'

'Dammit, man, we don't turn the police force inside out for "remote possibilities". I think it's about time we reviewed this case,' he said. He marched into interview room one. 'Tell Jock to put Bishop down,' he said to me. He sat behind his desk, and now he looked like a worried schoolmaster rather than

Buddha.

Jock came in and took Bishop away. Sir William, who'd sensed the changed atmosphere, got up, ready to leave. 'I'd like you to stay, Sir William, if you can?'

Sir William looked at his watch. Every minute that passed he was earning money, I thought, but dismissed that as uncharitable. He seemed to have a genuine interest in Bishop, just as Dr Gervis had been interested. Just as I was interested. The only two men who paid no regard to Bishop as a human being were Pope and the chief inspector. They, of course, were the hierarchy, the men who wrote the rules that other men like Jackson and I had to obey, the rules under which the Bishops of this world suffered. Because, with few exceptions, men like Jackson and I had to go on risk to defy those rules, jeopardizing our very existence. When a man builds up a home, a position, a family . . . Jackson had none of these things, of course, but, I reminded myself, I had. Often I thought that one day I'd say to hell with the police force, go out and find myself a steady job in some factory. One half of me knew I never would. I'm certain Sir William could explain that feeling to me, if ever I have the opportunity to ask him.

Seeing Pope sitting at the desk, with a lost look on his face, I felt compassion for him. There must have been days when he too wished he were employed anywhere but the police force. A man like Pope, dynamic, resourceful, could get a job anywhere. He was a natural leader, a born commander of men, but sitting there, imprisoned by the enormity of time, energy and effort he had unleashed on what were, after all, only a detective inspector's suppositions, he gave me a sense of pity and of personal shame.

'Look, Chief Superintendent,' I said, determined to make a clean breast of all my suspicions. I was going to tell him what I'd thought about the Sparkling Cleaning Company's contract, the possibility of Bishop having overheard a dialogue and from it constructing an improbable scheme to gain a million pounds.

He glared at me. 'Inspector Armstrong,' he said, 'take a radio car and go see how that daughter of yours is doing. And that's an order.' It was also a slap in the face, a get-out-of-my-sight dismissal with which I couldn't possibly argue.

'Very good, Chief Superintendent,' I said.

The chief inspector had followed us into the room; he was shaking his head as if one of his pets had been caught making a mess on the floor.

I went into the lobby. In the yard at the back of the station we keep two cars with radios, as well as several crew-manned cars that spend their days on patrols. Only one crew-manned car was there. I took the nearest of the other two cars, a green Ford Escort. Apart from the short aerial sticking from the centre of the roof, you couldn't tell it was a police car. As soon as I was driving along the High Street, I switched on the radiophone and called in. The car was Baker Baker Four.

At the end of the High Street I should have turned left for St Matthew's Hospital. I turned right towards Arlington Villas.

Mrs Calleja was sitting in the front room; a spider of a woman, large in body, but neat and fashionable. She was wearing modern spectacles, and her hair had recently been rinsed pink. Her nails, though on old hands, were blood-red, newly painted. Her skirt, twinset jumper, and cardigan were clean and well pressed. She saw me looking. 'I like to keep myself young,' she said. 'Life's an adventure if you take advantage of it.'

That wasn't bad for openers at seventy-five.

'Bishop has a friend,' I said. 'I'm trying to trace him. I think an adventurous lady like you might be able to help. I imagine nothing passes you by. . . .'

'He's never brought a girl here to spend the night,' she said. 'Apart from anything else, I wouldn't allow it. At my age you don't invite comparison . . .'

'Or competition . . . ?'

She laughed. 'I can see you and I are going to get on well,' she said. 'What a pity you're married. I could make a man of you. . . .'

I didn't ask how she knew I was married—I wasn't going to invite her to say I had a henpecked air. 'I wasn't necessarily meaning a *girl*, to spend the night . . .'

'A *boy*? Bishop wasn't queer, you know, or I wouldn't have wasted my time on him.'

'A visitor. Not to stay the night. Just to visit.'

'Ah, you must mean that man from the Labour Exchange. . . . Yes, he did have a friend who came four or five times. Bishop sent him away with a flea in his ear. I once overheard them say'—she saw the way I was looking. 'Yes, I'm not above spying on people when I want to. How else would I fill my life . . . ?'

'Or find material for those adventures . . . ?'

'Oh, yes, we *are* going to get on together. You're quick as a flash, aren't you, just like my late husband. . . .'

'The visitor. You overheard something . . .'

'And determined too. I like that in a man.'

'The visitor . . . ?'

'Bishop couldn't stand him. Practically threw him out each time. But the man came crawling back. I say man. He wasn't my type, you understand. Ugly, but not ugly enough to be beautiful and interesting, if you see what I mean. I like some ugly men. Clark Gable was ugly, so was Spencer Tracy. . . .'

'Any other visitor . . . ?'

'There was a boy . . .'

'What sort of boy . . . ?'

'Oh, what's that word they use, a callow youth. That's it, a callow youth. Came a couple of times. No, I'm telling a lie, he came three times. Each time it was the same story. Stand on the pavement for half an hour or more, making up his mind. I was worried, I can tell you. Sort of a hippie, but without the long hair and the beads. Then he'd call down the steps, "Mr Bishop, Mr Bishop." Soft-voiced lad . . .'

'But not queer . . . ?'

'No, not that sort of soft voice. Anyway, Bishop eventually would come to the door leading to the basement. And he'd say, very roughly, "What do you want . . . ?"'

'And the boy would say . . .'

'Galloping along, aren't we? The boy would say, "I've come to apologize. . . ."'

'And then Bishop would let him in?'

'Never! Bishop would say, "All right, you've apologized" and the boy would go away. Bishop always went out afterwards, and sometimes he'd stay out all night again.'

'You've no idea where?'

'Is that a statement . . .?'

'A question. . . .'

'I think I might know where. . . .'

'Where?'

'Can't you be a bit more friendly? Come and sit here beside me. I like talking to a man. I haven't had a real man to talk to for such a long time. Come and sit beside me. You needn't worry, I'm not going to seduce you. I could have at one time you know. Even though you're married. I could have had you in bed within half an hour. And kept you there! Now, what's that they say, it would take me all night to do what I used to do all night. . . .'

I sat where she indicated, on a footstool before her chair. She placed her hand on my head. Her touch was comforting, somehow, as if she'd been a masseuse.

'I'd like to stay and talk to you,' I said, 'because I don't often get a chance to meet an adventurous person like you, but alas, I don't have much time. I'm a police officer.'

'I know that. . . .'

'And I'm on a case, and I have to find Bishop's young friend. Quickly.'

'Thank you for the compliment,' she said. 'For that, I'm going to help you. I think I might know where Bishop's young friend might live. At the bottom of Arlington Grove is a house that has been condemned for years; they're going to pull it down when they start the Phase Four development of this area. It's a lot of nonsense, all this Phase One, Two and Three, but I won't waste your time by going into that. A group of young people live in that house. They're all mixed up, girls and boys. I know the police have been keeping an eye on them, but they do no harm. They don't take drugs or have wild parties or anything like that, apparently. They're just living rent free you might say. A woman called Mrs Tolly comes to clean for me. I can't stand her, she's a malicious gossip. One day she said, as soon as she arrived, bursting to tell me, "I saw your lodger going into that house in Arlington Grove!" I shut her up fast, wouldn't let her talk about my lodgers in that sort of way. I can only conclude the house she meant is the one at the bottom of Arlington Grove.'

She took her hand from my head. 'There, I haven't had the opportunity of talking with a real man for such a long time; I'm afraid I've rather let my tongue run away with me. Be gentle and kind with Mr Bishop, Inspector. He's a man more sinned against than sinning, if you can remember that old-fashioned phrase.'

I stood up and, on impulse, bent down again and kissed her on her cheek. Her skin was soft and smooth. 'Some people will never be old-fashioned,' I said.

She gurgled with delight, sounding rather like – what was her name, the TV person with Lord Popham? 'Bless you for that,' Mrs Calleja said. 'Now, go about your business. . . .'

When I got back to the Ford Escort I called in. They put me through to Jock and he spoke quietly. 'They've found a place like the one you said, Inspector. Now they're searching it.'

'Where is it?'

'Not far from Putney Bridge. Another of these brewery cellars only this one you get in from the top. There's a ladder. Part of the wall's been broached by the river over the years, and it fills up with the tide. Take the ladder away, and anybody you'd dropped in at low tide would swim about until they got too tired. The walls, apparently, are unclimbable. Smooth brickwork, covered in moss and algae. The watchman at the brewery knows about it because his dog once fell in and he had a hell of a job to get it out.'

'How's the chief superintendent?'

'Breathing fire and brimstone. He seems to have got the idea we're all on a wild goose chase. I think he regrets having gone for it in such a big way. He sent the P.R. team away, and he's had the money locked up in one of the cells.'

'And Bishop?'

'He's in the next cell. It must be driving him crazy to be so close and not able to touch it.'

'And Sir William?'

'He's left. The chief super said he didn't think there was any point in him staying around. If you ask me, he didn't want another witness in case the story should turn out to be wrong.'

'No trace of the yacht?'

'None. The weather's really closed in, apparently, all across the mouth of the Thames, round the coast from Harwich to Newhaven. Mist and fog both, and no wind to blow them away. No answer to the radio, but apparently they've found a man who crewed for Lord Wentworth at Cowes, and he said the radio was on the blink then. They stripped it out, and had it fixed after Cowes Week. They've been on to the firm who did the job. They say it *should* be all right. . . . They've had a chopper out from Manston, but he can't see a thing. I talked to the pilot myself. Apparently it's like dirty yellow cotton wool down there, that's how he described it.'

'So everything's going on all right, but nobody is asking for Inspector Armstrong.'

'That's right. If I were you, I'd get lost. For about a year, I'd say, looking at the chief super's face. . . .'

CHAPTER EIGHT

The house at the bottom of Arlington Grove was a typical terrace house of the 1920s period, 'front' room downstairs, kitchen-cum-dining room at the back where the family would normally live, scullery out at the back, lavatory in the yard, doubtless containing squares of torn up newspaper hanging from a nail. Shed in the back yard acting as a party wall with the house next door. Three bedrooms upstairs. In some parts of London such houses have been 'done up', bathrooms have been put in using a grant from the Council, the front doors have been panelled in hardboard and painted a vicious colour, and the houses sold as bijou residences for twenty times what it cost to build them. These were in the wrong part, and all the hardboard in the world wouldn't make desirable residences of them. They were destined to be pulled down to make room for a block of flats. In front of the house an apron about ten feet deep once had been a garden; now it was a patch of waist-high weeds, a lavatory for dogs.

The front door was open. I went in. Small hallway with the remains of a strip of linoleum. Door to the right, door straight ahead. *Monarch of the Glens* on the wall, its frame coloured by mildew, its glass fly-specked. I opened the door to the front room. The floor was covered by newspapers, blankets and what looked like sleeping bags. No furniture. Curtain at the window and a blanket hung on nails covered the lower half. Broken bulb in the light fitting, and the switch inside the door had been smashed.

The bundle of sleeping bags on the floor stirred. A face appeared. At least, I thought it was a face among the hair. I couldn't tell if it was a male or female. Eyes opened, looked at me. 'Hello, fuzz,' a voice said lazily and the face disappeared again, burrowing back into the pile of cloth.

I walked to the back of the hallway and opened the kitchen door. A table in the centre, covered with tins of what had been Ideal milk. Now the tins were used as ashtrays and drinking mugs. Old-fashioned grate, with the ashes of sticks in it. I felt the hood; it was still warm. Sink in the corner, half-full of water on which a scum of grease floated. Frying pan on the draining board, two sausages, and a cardboard box that advertised 'Fresh, fresh, fresh, Hamburgers'. I didn't believe it. I heard the sound of the chain being pulled in the outside lavatory; the lavatory door opened and a girl appeared in the yard. She was wearing jeans and a heavy fishermen's knit sweater. She would need that. The house felt and smelled cold, damp with the sweat and breath from a legion of bodies. Everything was covered in a film of greasy dust, the city grime of years of neglect. She came into the kitchen and showed no surprise when she saw me. I'd say she was about twenty-six and she looked clean, her hair obviously brushed. Her eyes were bright and alive and she seemed to walk purposefully.

'Hi!' she said. 'Who are you?'

'Inspector Armstrong.'

'Oh, the fuzz.' In her mouth the word wasn't offensive, just a description she was used to. 'What can I do for you? Is anything wrong?'

'Do you know a boy called Peter?'

'I know a lot of boys called Peter. Can you tell me anything about him.'

'He's the friend of a man called Bishop.'

'Oh, Peckham Pete! What's he done?'

'Nothing, so far as I know. I just want to talk to him.'

'He hasn't been around for a couple of days. They come, they go, I don't keep a check. Anyway, come upstairs, we can't talk here.'

We climbed the stairs and came to an upper landing off which were three bedroom doors, all open. The floors were covered as the one downstairs, but in the corners of two of them I could see a couple of old flock mattresses. Lumps in the flock suggested where bodies might be. A fourth door was closed. She used the keys from the pocket of her jeans to open it and we went up into an attic. In comparison to the rest of the house this place was spotless. Its floor was covered by an old carpet; there were a desk and chair beneath the dormer window and at the other end of the room a proper single bed made up with sheets and blankets.

'I call this the office,' she said, 'and we have an agreement that nobody comes up here without an invitation.' Her voice was quiet and in it I could hear a suggestion of a broad Midlands accent. She saw me looking around and laughed. 'You're surprised, aren't you?' I had to admit I was. 'Down below,' she said, 'is what the kids want when they come here. Up here is the bourgeois respectability they're escaping from. Okay, so I'm a bit of a phoney but I can't take too much of it down there. I have to get away up here sometimes.'

I was puzzled by the set-up, wondering at Bishop's involvement.

'We keep open house,' she said. 'The kids come, the kids go. I try to provide somewhere they can sleep because that's all most of them want to do, sleep. . . .'

'. . . and escape from reality?'

'Wouldn't you if you were a kid? I don't allow drugs or anything like that. I let the kids stay and any that seem to linger on, well, I find them a job.'

'Sort of Labour Exchange.'

'Are you joking? Old Mrs Marston up the road, arthritic, pensioner, needs her garden done. A man wants help putting up a fence. You'd be surprised how many jobs there are if you go looking for them. Half the time we get paid. It's a first step for the kids. Gives them a sense of belonging. They turn over the cash, we buy food and cigarettes.'

'And booze?'

'Don't knock it!'

'I'm just asking questions. Does it have a name?'

'Most of the kids are running away from names. Call it the Self-Help Society and tell your people to stop turning us over. If the owner turns up, we'll pay rent if he wants it.' She looked defiantly at me. 'I keep records,' she said. 'Do you know that in the last three months twelve per cent of all the kids who came here went back home! We need a lot more places like this. Trouble is, if they were official people would start putting in iron beds and painting the walls green and white and sticking up notices.'

I knew I had to hear her out before I would get any response about Bishop and Peckham Pete. I'd come here with all the strikes against me. I was the fuzz, I'd washed my face and shaved and that made me one of *them*.

'What's *your* name?' I asked.

'Megan Davies. I know that sounds Welsh but I was born and brought up in Northampton. You can check on me. They must be used to getting inquiries about me by now. No previous arrests, no form. The headmistress at Northampton Girls High School will tell you I always did like poking my nose into other people's business. Now I make a full-time job of it. It's better than bashing a typewriter for some guy who sells shoes, or makes nuts and bolts.'

'All right,' I said, 'let's call a truce! I take you at your face value; you take me at mine. Is it a deal? I'm looking for Peckham Pete as you call him because I think he can help me by giving information about a man called Bishop. You've obviously met Bishop since you weren't surprised when I mentioned his name. Can you tell me anything about Bishop?'

'Bishop, that's the man called Jim isn't it? He's been here a few times. The day I got that desk they dumped off the horse cart by the front gate, Jim Bishop was walking past and I asked him to give me a lift in with it. He was a bit crabby at first but then helped me. Next time he was passing he brought me some books. I made him a cup of coffee. The kids were arguing in the kitchen and he joined in. If you ask me he's just a lonely fellow, wanted to talk to somebody. The only thing I've noticed is that if by accident anybody gets on to anything personal, he'll go. Him and Pete seemed to take a liking to each other – they aren't bent or anything – and without trying to be an amateur psychiatrist I'd say that Pete is looking for a father figure and Jim Bishop wants a son. It got so that Jim Bishop stayed here a couple of nights. I even sent him out on a couple of odd jobs. He once fixed an electric iron for a woman down the road and earned us fifty pence.'

'Good in electrical things, is he?' I asked, still thinking about time bomb fuses.

She laughed. 'He got the red wire where the green wire ought to be and the first time the lady used the iron it blew out the main fusebox.'

I looked at my watch. 'You in a hurry or something?' she asked.

'Yes, I am.'

When she spoke again her voice had a bitter edge to it. 'Not much time left in the world is there, for hearing about people's problems, people's inadequacies, people's little failures. I reckon the best thing I do here is just simply to listen to the kids, to let them talk. Okay, what's your problem?'

I decided to come straight out with it. Megan Davies probably knew Bishop as well as anybody if she'd spent so much time listening to him.

'What can you tell me about Bishop and Pete?' I asked. 'Do you think they could be involved together in a kidnapping?'

'Oh, so that's it, eh? No wonder you don't have any time. They were very close. Look, I'll tell you something. One time Pete brought a shotgun here. I don't know where he got it but I made him take it away quick. That's all we need for the do-gooders to close us down. Pete is easily led and he'll do anything for Jim Bishop. If there's any trouble you can guess Jim Bishop has led Pete into it.'

'Has there been trouble?'

She shook her head. 'Not here,' she said, 'I keep a pretty close eye on what goes on. But I do know they go somewhere together.'

'Where?'

'I don't know. Sometimes Bishop comes here and wakes Pete up. "Shall we go," he'll say as if it's all arranged. Maybe it's a job. Maybe they go to the pictures. Who knows?'

'Let me ask you a straight question. Do you think Bishop is capable of kidnapping someone, or not?'

She thought for a long time while the clock ticked inexorably on. 'Yes,' she said, 'I do.'

CHAPTER NINE

I went back to the station. When I got there I hurried across the lobby hoping to get down to the cells before Chief Superintendent Pope saw me, but the door to interview room one opened and he was standing there.

'Inspector Armstrong,' he said. His voice should have shattered every pane of glass in the building.

I followed him inside and closed the door behind me. Jock was standing in the other doorway and when he saw me he withdrew like a rabbit going into a burrow when it hears the first shotgun being fired.

'Sit down,' Chief Superintendent Pope said. 'We've now found three places that conform to your specification. We've been down into each one with frogmen and underwater lights and draghooks but we haven't found a single thing except the body of a tramp, who'd obviously fallen into a hole by mistake. How does that strike you?' he asked, deceptively calm.

I couldn't think of anything to say other than, 'Sir William was wrong. Bishop *did* have a friend.'

'Then he was a damned sight luckier than you, because I guarantee that when this business is over *you* won't have a friend! Do you realize the enormity of what you've done?' he asked. 'Do you realize just how many people have become involved in this case?'

I couldn't guess, but it had to be in the hundreds. I looked at my watch again: half past four. One hour to the half hour deadline.

'I think I might have something, Chief Superintendent!' I said. 'Bishop did have a friend and at one time the friend had a shotgun. They used to go off somewhere together, just the two of them. . . .' My voice trailed away.

'Go on, Inspector, I'm waiting for you, waiting for you to give me one piece of relevant information. Just one piece, that's all I ask!'

'The shotgun . . .?' I said desperately.

'I have a friend,' Pope said. 'He has a shotgun. It's a Purdey. It belonged to his grandfather. Does that make my friend a kidnapper? What we've heard today is the biggest load of non-information, of claptrap, that it's ever been my misfortune to listen to! As for the commissioner, well, if he doesn't have an apoplectic fit I shall be very surprised. I daren't go back to Scotland Yard because I know that when I do they'll laugh me out of the building. I believe that Prince Charles is on that yacht and the radio is on the blink. I personally have spoken to the man who repaired it two months ago and he tells me that although it was working perfectly when he came off the boat he can't guarantee it hasn't broken down again. Just as soon as this fog lifts we've got a helicopter standing by that will hover over that boat. What Prince Charles will say I have no way of knowing, but I imagine he's learned one or two fruity words while serving in the Navy.'

'You're not going to pay Bishop the money in an hour's time?'

'That's not for you or me to say, Inspector. That's a matter for the Royal Family.'

'So they, at least, are taking it seriously.'

'Seriously? Of course they're taking it seriously. We're all taking it seriously. It's my private conviction that when we get through to that yacht I for one am going to have to resign. That's how seriously I'm taking it!'

'Can I go and see Bishop, Chief Superintendent?'

'Detective Inspector Armstrong, so far as I'm concerned you can go to Hell . . . !'

I went downstairs to the cells, expecting to find Bishop cowed by being there; instead he was chipper. He'd been chatting with Cockney Alf, a man who could get words out of a stone.

'When are they going to charge me, Inspector?' Alf said when he saw me.

'They'll get around to you. . . .'

'It's a dead liberty. Do they think I've got all the time in the world . . . ?'

'We've had things to do. . . .'

The constable let me into Bishop's cell. He was sitting on the side of the bed and didn't get up. 'Only an hour left, Inspector!'

he said.

'Don't you get cheeky. Alf has privileges. He earns them by talking to us when we need him.' I sat on the only chair in the cell; the constable locked me in and closed the outer door to give us privacy.

'No comfortable interview room this time?' Bishop said.

'Like I said, don't get cheeky.' He'd found a new confidence from somewhere; perhaps it came from the knowledge that we were taking him seriously as an individual, that we no longer let him sit in the corner of the room while we talked around him. Here I'd have to talk to him. 'I hear you're a dab hand at mending electric irons,' I said. That would do for openers.

'You found Megan Davies.' It wasn't a question.

'That wasn't so difficult. Like the chief superintendent said, we shall find most of the things we want to know by detective work. Like drops of water, going through a stone.'

'In time.'

'We can go faster when we need to. People help the police, you know. Most people trust us.'

'I'm not most people.'

'I've been thinking about you. About you being taken prisoner in the war and tortured and all that. You know, you're a phoney! I asked myself, how many other people in wars were captured and tortured? The answer is, a hell of a lot. Yet, it's a funny thing, we never hear from most of them. Most of them have had the guts to settle down into normal life, take a job and hang on to it, work and earn some kind of living for themselves instead of trying to sponge off the rest of us. Most of them would recoil with loathing at the thought of capturing another man and subjecting him to the sort of imprisonment they had themselves. I think you're a phoney, Jim Bishop!'

That wiped the smile off his face, as if he'd sucked a lemon. I'd handled him the wrong way from the start. Offering him help, going out of my way to make life more easy for him, thinking of introducing him to Nancy, finding a room for him. If he'd wanted, if he'd played ball by letting Mrs Calleja talk to him from time to time, he could have had a comfortable home all these years. There were a lot of worse places than that basement room. Mrs Calleja would have looked after him in her own way. She, too, was a lonely person because of her age; but she had the interest and personality to make life pleasant for a man like Bishop. Jackson went out of his way to walk round to Bishop's lodgings to see why he'd reneged on the job; Megan Davies, no doubt, provided little jobs for him when he wanted them and an open door. Because the marks of Bishop's scars were visible, we'd all been conned into giving him more sympathy and care than he deserved. We were the ones who'd made him what he was, the ones who'd suffered a feeling of self-guilt every time we'd looked at those scarred hands.

'You've made quite a habit of opening your shirt and showing your scars, haven't you?' I said. ' "Don't hurt me, don't touch me, be kind to me, because I've been tortured." Well I have news for you, Mr Bishop. I'm not affected by the sight of your scars any more! So far as I'm concerned, you're just another customer. Just another case, like Cockney Alf along there. The only difference between you is that Cockney Alf is a straight criminal. He knows what he is and asks no sympathy for it. He chooses to make his life that way, a few months outside, a few months inside, and that's his affair. It's not my job to *care* about him. All I have to do is catch him, and see he gets to court on time. So far as I'm concerned, the same goes for you. I'll catch you too, and see that you get to court on time. I'm going to try to find Prince Charles. If I do, we'll charge you with kidnapping. If he's on the yacht after all, we'll charge you with "interfering", but if he has been hidden by you, if he dies, we'll charge you with murder.'

'In an hour you have to give me the money and let me go. The commissioner said so.'

'We'll do that too, if the commissioner says so. We'll give you the money, stand on the front steps and wave you goodbye. But once you've got away, and we've rescued Prince Charles, I'll come after you, even if I have to resign from the police force to do it.'

Though I may have seemed supremely confident to him, inside myself I was cursing. I'd really blown it now I'd let my temper run away with me. I was fed up to the back teeth with the attitude of people towards me, the feeling around the station that once again Inspector Armstrong had made a fool of himself, and in the process had involved the mighty forces of the law. I'd seen the smirk on Sergeant Jones's face as I'd crossed the lobby, the way Jock had looked at me as if to say, 'you poor bastard', the attitude of the chief superintendent. The courts say – beyond any possibility of doubt. That phrase and the idea it incorporates are the foundation stone of our legal system. We have to work with it. Beyond any possible doubt. There was a doubt, wasn't there? Bishop *could* be telling the truth, couldn't he? It was possible for him to have kidnapped Prince Charles. If he'd had Peckham Pete's shotgun concealed in one of the vans the Sparkling Cleaning Company used. When the prince and his detective came into the mews to get out the car, they'd be relaxed after the night's sleep, not expecting trouble at that hour of morning. It would be easy to level the shotgun, say 'get in here quickly'. With a shotgun pointing at the prince, the detective wouldn't dare jump. He'd wait for a better opportunity. Pete could sit there, holding the shotgun, while Bishop drove. Or Pete, presumably, could drive. That brick hole in the ground would have suited very well. Out of the van, into the hole. Probably somewhere they could hang on to at low water, but nowhere they could go as the water rose. It was all *possible*. But now I'd blown my last chance of cooperation from Bishop by losing my temper.

'I know all about Peckham Pete,' I said, 'and where you go together. . . .'

Now Bishop was shaking his head and smiling at me. 'No, Inspector,' he said, 'it won't wash. If you knew all about *Peckham Pete* – and what a silly name that is! – and where we go together, you wouldn't be in here, would you, threatening me with personal revenge. You'd be out there, browbeating Peter! If you think I'm a truculent person, wait until you meet him. I'll talk to you all you want about Peter. He's a product of our society, too. He doesn't realize it but he's being tortured just as I was, but not in physical ways. They used to jeer at me, squatting naked in that pit, laughing at my manhood, at the size of my parts, telling me how much I stank. Nowadays, society achieves the same results in more subtle and therefore more vicious ways. By hinting, by suggesting, that if we don't use their wonder products no one will ever want to be in a room with us because of the odour, we'll never have a successful life because of our inadequacies. It doesn't bother me, because I'm past all that, but young boys like Peter, they really care when they see, perhaps unconsciously, an advert on television, in all the papers, saying perhaps they are failing as *men* because they don't use Boggo. All those adverts that cast doubt on a man's basic integrity are torturing lads like Peter.'

'You have all the theories,' I said, 'but perhaps if you spent more time working to earn a living you'd be less able to feel sorry for drop-outs like Peter and yourself. Because that's what you are, though you may not accept the idea. You like to think of yourself as a war-victim, but to me you've just become a drop-out. I met your Mrs Calleja and Megan Davies. In their own way, those two people are trying to solve problems similar to yours. Mrs Calleja maintains her self-respect by keeping herself neat and tidy and interested in what's going on about her. Megan Davies does it by caring actively for other people, providing a home of sorts, helping them see they can have a place in life. Life as it is lived, not some warped and twisted image like the one you carry around with you.'

'You've changed, Inspector. . . .'

'I know I have. I changed when I met those two people, when I saw the trap I was falling into with you. You almost had me believing that, because you'd had a raw deal, you merited extra care and sympathy. Look, Bishop, the Korean War was over a long time ago. The sooner you accept that, the sooner you start to live life as it now is, the better you'll be. Because there aren't too many Jacksons about who'll come running round every time you fail to turn up for a job.'

'Jackson, Jackson. I hate him. . . .'

I was surprised by the vehemence with which he spoke.

'I hate him. He's the one who caused me most bother. Sending me to jobs I couldn't do. Creeping round to my place, hectoring me, saying why didn't I stay on the job, telling me there'd be no more jobs if I didn't stick to them. And always snivelling about his own situation, about how they hadn't given him promotion, how he never had anybody to talk to, how they stole his pens and never gave them back.'

'Jackson was too close to your own image of yourself, wasn't he? A lonely man who couldn't really cope. I can see why you'd hate him.'

'So wise, aren't you. Of course you are. You can be, just as Jackson could be. You've got it made. Good jobs, good pay, no doubt good places to live. . . .'

'Good places? Don't make me laugh. Jackson lives in digs, lodgings, a boarding house. But he sticks with his job, just as I stick with mine. You never stick. You always walk away.'

He cradled his head in his hands, as if he wanted to shut out the sound of my voice. Without taking his hands away he looked across the cell at me.

'I tried,' he said, 'honestly I tried, in the beginning. When I came out of hospital, they gave me a job. In an office. Filing papers. Every time I went to a girl's desk to take the letters away for filing, I'd see her look at my hands and shiver. It wasn't my fault. We had a canteen, but nobody would sit with me. I overheard one of the girls say "It puts me off my food, just to look at his hands!" It was as if somebody had exploded a bomb inside my head. Honest! I walked out of that place but I don't remember leaving. I walked about for hours and hours, hearing that stupid little bitch's voice. It took the best part of a week to get over it. When I went back, they'd given the job away. They didn't want to take me on again, although I knew that they were short of people. When I went back to the Labour Exchange, as it then was, they played hell with me for walking off the job. I couldn't get any unemployment money. The man told me to apply for Supplementary Benefits, but they wouldn't give me anything because I had no dependants. That's how it's gone on ever since. I try a job, screw my courage up to settle down, but always somebody says something that sets me off.'

'You should have gone to the hospital to apply for medical treatment. They'd have seen you all right.'

'I did, I did. They were very efficient. I told them what had happened to me and they arranged for me to see a psychiatrist. He spent an hour listening to me and all he could say was, "Look, you must learn to forget about your hands and the way your face looks. Or you'll get a complex about it." A *complex*. . . . I'd tried hard to be normal, to behave in a normal way.

Apparently I was *too* normal for the psychiatrist. I didn't show any signs of madness. According to him, I wasn't crazy enough for him. If I had been crazy, a gibbering idiot, he would have bothered to sit down with me and see what he could do. But because I held myself under control, he wasn't interested. One time a welfare worker who came to see me, an amateur woman, a do-gooder, suggested privately that I should put my hands round a policeman's throat. Then, she suggested, they'll lock you up and see you get treatment. I told her she was a monster for even suggesting such a thing. She took the huff and I never saw her again. I didn't miss her. She was a dabbler.'

'And this kidnapping . . .?'

'I became fed up of being eternally without money and at the mercy of the "dabblers". That man Jackson was a dabbler, coming round to my place, playing the amateur psychiatrist. What could he know? The only thing he was fit for was shovelling people into different jobs. Peter and I dream about what we'll do with a lot of money. Oh, not the sort of things you might imagine. We don't want motor cars or yachts or wardrobes of fancy clothes. We just want to be free to travel about wherever we want, whenever we want, without being subjected to interrogation by these "dabblers". We want to use the money to get away from them.'

'You'll take Peter with you?'

'He's helped me. . . .'

'He's standing guard for you. . . .'

'You might say that. . . .'

'You must have chuckled when the doctors said you were a loner. . . .'

'I could hardly keep a straight face. If they want to believe that, so much the better. But, I could tell *you* didn't believe it. And then, all that business about a bomb. . . .'

'You would never bother with a bomb. Too indirect for you.'

'You're absolutely right.'

'Anyway, you don't need a bomb with Peter's shotgun. . . .'

'How did you know about that? Oh, yes, Megan Davies must have told you that.'

'Peter's a good driver, is he?'

I'd gone that whisker too far. So far, I'd been able to avoid using a direct question. I'd been holding my breath lest he realized how much he was telling me and now, in my anxiety to get ahead, in my fear that time was running out, I'd strayed over that invisible boundary again.

'Driver? Peter?'

'I was thinking, if you want to visit some of these far away places it'd be useful to take a spare driver with you. I once drove on my holiday all the way down through France. My wife can't drive. It'd have been very helpful if she could have taken the wheel from time to time, like perhaps Peter could. . . .'

It was no use. He'd clammed up again.

When I went upstairs, Parkins and Milner were both standing by the desk, and from the curious way they looked, sort-of ill-at-ease, I guessed Sergeant Jones had been talking about me. Parkins came across the lobby.

'Bad news from the Intensive Care Unit at the hospital,' he said. 'The worst!'

They say your heart stops still. Mine did. It was suddenly as if the blood stood still in my arteries, as if the last breath I had drawn was beyond memory. 'Oh, God,' I said, thinking immediately not about my daughter but about Sarah. What a rotten thing I'd done to her, to leave her alone all this time to face what was happening. My poor darling Sarah. Tears came to my eyes but I was thinking still of my wife, not my daughter.

'It's always hell for the wife,' I said.

Parkins nodded. Milner came over and held my arm. 'Try not to take on so, Bill,' he said, 'perhaps it was for the best. Better to die quickly than be a cripple for the rest of your life.'

A cripple? Surely peritonitis couldn't do that to a child?

Parkins took the handkerchief from my top pocket and offered it to me. 'I didn't know you were so close, Bill,' he said, 'I hadn't realized you cared quite so much. . . .'

'Of course I *cared*,' I said. 'Just because I spend most of my time here, when I could be at home. Just because I take the time to do what I have to, it doesn't mean I don't care. . . .'

'I suppose not,' he said, surprised. 'But I'll be honest with you. I thought you and Adams didn't go much on each other. I remember you were daggers drawn over that business with the clock. I thought he blamed you for blocking his promotion to super. . . .'

'Adams?' I shouted, 'who the hell are we talking about?'

'Inspector Adams. He died, in the Intensive Care Unit,' Inspector Parkins said, bewildered.

I began to laugh. 'I thought you meant, I thought you meant the one who was dead was my daughter. My daughter!'

'Oh, Christ,' he said, 'I forgot you were still waiting to hear. . . . You can't have seen the message Sergeant Jones has . . .'

'What message . . .?'

I pushed them aside in my anxiety to get to the desk. Sergeant Jones handed me a piece of paper. He could just as easily have told me what was on it. 'Doctor says Helen all right now. Gone home, but will stop somewhere and have a bite to eat because I'm starving!'

'She telephoned about five minutes ago,' the sergeant said. 'I offered to fetch you from the cells, but she said don't bother him!'

Parkins was standing at my elbow. 'Bill,' he said, 'I'm really sorry. That must have been a bloody awful shock for you, I mean, thinking I was talking about your daughter. . . .'

'Forget,' I said, 'forget it.' The news from Sarah had so cheered me. I hadn't realized quite how worried I'd been about Helen, deep inside. 'We'll have to take a collection for Mrs Adams,' I said. 'Who's going to do it? Jones?'

He always did. Situated by the front door, he was ideally placed. And he had the right sort of face and solemn manner.

'Anybody been asking for me?' I said, meaning the chief superintendent.

'Nobody! Unless you count these fifteen people.' He handed me a list of telephone calls; all had to do with other cases I was working on.

'No, I don't count them. . . .'

'Don't let this *Royal* business go to your head, Inspector, will you?'

'No, I won't.'

I looked at the clock above the desk. It was taken throughout the station as the official timekeeper; we set our watches by it when we came in.

Where could Pete be? Had he been left in charge of Prince

Charles and the detective, both dropped into a hole somewhere? Normally we could find him. We could send out a message for the police to search every likely spot within the whole area. We've done it before. Flash a photograph about. Have you seen this man? Oddly enough, it works. There are always people who say, yes, he comes along every Tuesday at ten o'clock, he walks his dog on to the Common, he rides his bicycle past here. But that takes time, and time was running away. Fifty minutes left. Less than an hour. And I was wasting it.

Back to the Ford Escort. I didn't bother to ask for permission to leave the station. Okay, so they'd have my knackers. I was past caring. Five minutes to drive to the house in Arlington Grove. Traffic was bad and once I overtook on the pavement. People cursing. If they'd known it was a police car they'd have waved me through.

Megan Davies was in the kitchen. She'd washed the pots, relighted the fire, bought a mountain of sausages and packets of hamburgers. 'It's all they'll eat,' she said when she saw me looking. The kitchen looked brighter with the fire going. 'They sleep all day,' she said, 'some of them. It's almost as if they arrived here in shock. When they finally wake up, a third go home again. A third drift off somewhere else. A third stay for a while.'

'Who knows Pete best?' I asked.

She thought about it. 'Pete's been here longer than most. On and off. I suppose Larry knows him as well as anybody.'

'Where's Larry?'

'In the front room, asleep. He works nights. Washing up and preparing vegetables. He earns good money. Here's something for your social anthology,' she said defiantly, 'he gives it all to me. That's how I bought these sausages.'

I was already halfway out of the kitchen. 'You're full of surprises,' I said as I went down the hall.

Larry was the hairy bundle I'd seen when I first came into the house. I picked the rags off him, nauseated by the smell. He sat up, wiping his eyes. Hair seemed to sprout from every part of his head except the cheekbones below his eyes, all knitted together in a mop that flopped down around his neck and ears. Even his eyebrows were long and hung over his eyes like those of a collie dog. He was wearing a woollen roll-neck sweater and corduroy trousers, with sea boot stockings drawn over them. He sat upright and fumbled in his trousers pocket, producing a bent packet of Gauloises Disques Bleu. I held out a lighted match.

'Thanks,' he said. His voice was American or Canadian. 'What can I do for you, officer?' he said, his voice cold but not uninterested.

'Megan tells me you know Pete, Peckham Pete.'

'I know him.'

We both heard footsteps coming down the hall. Megan came in carrying two drinking glasses full of coffee. Hot, strong, and sweet, though the milk was tinned. 'I reckoned you'd both need that,' she said. What did the Americans call such girls. 'Den-mothers?'

'Sure, I know Pete,' he said, when he'd taken a mouthful of coffee and another couple of puffs of his cigarette.

'Do you know Jim Bishop?'

He nodded.

'They go off together, occasionally. Do you know where?'

Now he was fully awake, and wary.

'Who wants to know. . . .?'

'Police inquiry. . . .'

'Yes, but like, what . . .?'

He struggled into the sitting position, his back against the wall. His eyes, or what I could see of them, were wary.

'I want to find Pete, to ask him a few questions.'

'About Bishop . . .?'

'I can't tell you any more.'

'In that case,' he said, 'that makes two of us.'

He started to get up, but never made it. I swung my arm in a short jab that punched into the pit of his stomach. He sat back against the wall, a surprised look on his face. He was gasping for breath. 'That hurt, copper!' he said.

'It was meant to hurt, to let you know I don't have time for games. Where will I find Pete? Where do he and Bishop go together?'

'I don't like being hurt, copper . . .!'

'Nobody does. It's a sad and realistic part of life. We all get hurt sometime. Where's Pete? Where do he and Bishop go?'

'And if I don't tell you?'
'You'll get hurt again.'

His mind was equating pain with pride. 'I was questioned by the fuzz but I didn't tell them anything!' It's a foolish meaningless pride. There's no honour in keeping your mouth closed. He'd learn that the hard way, fast. They call me the Thumper, okay. Sometimes I have to deal with people who only respect violence. Pain is a short-cut. I hate it, they hate it, but when I have to, I use it.

He tried to get up again, tried to push himself off that carpet of cloth in one spring, and that was a mistake. I chopped the inside of the elbow and his braced arm bent like a hinge with the force of the blow and his funny bone cracked against the wall as he slumped down again. He howled with pain.

There were rapid footsteps down the corridor from the kitchen and Megan Davies appeared in the doorway.

'What the devil do you think you're doing?' she said. 'You can't come in here hitting people.'

'You keep out of this,' I said.

Her eyes flashed anger at me. 'I will not,' she said. 'You pig!'

'He's one of the vicious ones,' Larry said from the floor.

'Right now,' I said, 'I'm in a hurry. I don't have time to be a nice guy anymore.'

'That's what you all say,' she said bitterly.

Larry was no fool. 'Okay, copper,' he said. 'Just for once I'm prepared to believe what you say. I don't want to be thumped again. Maybe I'm a coward.'

'You don't have to tell him a thing,' Megan said hotly. 'If he wants to ask questions there's a way of doing it and you have rights. You can tell him to piss off if you want to.'

He stopped rubbing his elbow and held up his hand.

'Hang on, Megan,' he said. 'Cool it. What's the question, copper? Where do Jim Bishop and Pete go. What do I give a shit where they go. Look, I work at the bottom of Arlington Street in that new Arlington Towers Hotel. All night. Sometimes I take a break outside to smoke a cigarette. I've seen them come past sometimes. In both directions. Once I saw them come past and they were having an argument. They came back about ten minutes later still arguing. That's all I know. Don't waste your time hitting me again if you're in such a hurry because I don't know anything else. No matter how much you hit me.'

'I'll be back,' I said.

'You won't find me. You've bust this place for me, copper.'

'When I come back I'll tell you why I thumped you.' I couldn't leave the room just like that. 'Look,' I said, 'don't go, wait here for me and I'll be back.'

Megan walked down the hall after me and her voice when she spoke was bitter and full of contempt. 'Larry is a good man,' she said, 'and a big help to me in what I'm trying to do here. Now you've screwed that up. If only you people would realize that all we want is to be left alone.'

'I'll be back,' I said as I walked down the path towards my car.

'Don't bother, copper!' She slammed the door.

It took me four minutes to get to the back of the Arlington Towers Hotel in a street that curved away from the main Arlington Road. I parked the car and sat thinking, visualizing the neighbourhood as it had been when I was a young copper, remembering the various jobs I'd done around there. It was a hotchpotch neighbourhood in the middle of re-developments. When I'd first come here it was full of small Victorian terrace houses; most of them had been pulled down and the area re-developed. There were several hotels of which the Arlington Towers was the largest. There'd been talk for years about razing the whole neighbourhood and even restructuring the lay-out of the streets. I started the engine and drove the car aimlessly around, street by street. Now that Peckham Pete had come into the picture everything had changed. Together the two of them could have taken the prince and his detective anywhere in this neighbourhood. There was no point in thinking any more about 'natural phenomena'.

People on the streets everywhere moving purposefully through the evening, going home to tea, supper, television, an evening of loneliness. Cars and taxis trundling along; everybody except me moving with a purpose. The shops were still open, of course, and all had someone in them, last minute customers hurrying before the six o'clock closing time. I drove round the back streets. They could be anywhere. Half an hour to go before the commissioner would be told whether to hand over the money or not. Pope, of course, would stay in the station until the last minute, constantly trying the radio link with the yacht, hoping to hear the sound of Prince Charles's voice. Would they pay out the money? It was impossible to know. I imagined the notes had all been marked in some way – that was standard procedure – and probably those two canvas suitcases weren't as innocent as they looked. It sounds a bit James Bondish but it's very easy to fix a bleep transmitter with which you can track someone's progress. Only a sick man would think he could walk away from a police station with a million pounds and not be tracked. Dammit, we could put a man on every rooftop with a radio and Bishop would never know he was being watched. We have a system of car surveillance that works very well; the following car is never actually visible to the suspect. We call it leap-frogging. I didn't believe the commissioner had been sitting there twiddling his thumbs. He'd have arranged a foolproof method of making sure that when the right time came we could pounce on Bishop and get that money back. But that wouldn't tell him where Prince Charles was!

I crawled down the seedy streets past rows of parked cars, past houses with curtain patterns that told of multiple occupancy. The streets were sour with the lost hopes of the people forced by circumstances to live there, moving each morning to some banal job, back each evening to hardboard partitions and rental furnishings.

At the end of the row, one house, no curtains, newspaper stuck to the inside of the window with cellotape. A rusty pram in what once had been the garden; a back drive shielded from view by a wooden fence eight feet high, the front door reinforced by galvanized iron. I drove down the back. No one could see me there. A rusting fridge near the back door, a cooker caked with grease. A cat watched me get out of the car; his hair stiffened and he growled; he was holding his front paw on a rat whose back was bent at an angle. I wasn't going to steal it from him. The back door was open an inch. I pushed it with my fingers, it swung wide. Inside, the back kitchen had the golden glow of a chapel as the last of the day's sun filtered through the yellowed newspaper stuck to the pane. Water had dripped from the ceiling and great gobs of plaster filled the stone sink. On the wall above a green plastic breadbin somebody had pencilled 'Don't forget to buy bread.'

I went through the house slowly, room by room. All the ceilings were down. Not even a tramp would live here.

The door of the front room was closed. I turned the handle and pushed gently; it would not move. I put my ear to the panel. Inside I could hear a murmuring which stopped abruptly. I stayed perfectly still for two minutes or possibly three; the murmuring started again. I stood back from the door, my hand on the handle, and slammed forward taking the force on the upper arm and my right shoulder. The door burst inwards and I was over the threshold and crouched in the room before the door banged back against the wall. There was a sudden shout and a bloodcurdling shriek, legs flying in all directions and claws extending towards my face as one of them jumped and I smelled the foetid stink and saw the remains they'd been devouring in the centre of the room as the cats spat, shrieked, sprang through the doorway, through the broken window through which the pigeons must have come in, the fat London pigeons trapped here by the marauding feline gang. I went out of the house, back into the car and reversed out of the drive as quickly as I could, shaken by that banshee screeching.

CHAPTER TEN

A man was selling newspapers at a road junction two minutes away from the back of the Arlington Towers Hotel. His red metal stand was propped against the wall and he sat beside it on a bentwood chair on which he'd placed a cushion.

'Have you been here long?' I asked him.

'Since half past four, governor.'

'I didn't mean today. I meant in general.'

'Do I know you?' he asked.

'No,' I said.

'Then what's it got to do with you how long I've been here?'

'Don't be shirty, mate. I'm only asking a question.'

'Fair enough. I've been here fifteen years, three times a day. I come out in the morning to catch 'em going to work, I'm out at dinner time, and I get 'em coming home. That answer your question?'

A man walked past and picked up an *Evening Standard*. The newspaper-seller took his money and said 'God bless you governor, mind how you go!'

He turned back to me. 'Ask him,' he said, 'if you want to know. He's been buying an *Express* in the morning and a *Standard* in the afternoon for as long as I can remember.'

I described Bishop to him wishing I had a photograph. You'd think they'd give us a polaroid camera but we have to get one from the stores and it's more bother than it's worth. 'You'd see him walking with a young lad.' I had no description of Pete and cursed myself for not having obtained one from Megan Davies, or Larry.

'A lot of people answer that description round here,' he said. 'What time of day might I be likely to see them?'

'Anytime.'

'Ah, well, I'm not here after half past nine till twelve o'clock and from half past one to half past four. I mean, it's not worth my while down here. I'd be lucky if I picked up enough to buy me a cup of tea in the off-peak.'

'But in the hours while you are here . . .?'

He thought; a couple of people came past and absent-mindedly he gave them the paper he knew they always took; I could see his was a regular clientele, day in, day out. I would have thought he was just the man to notice a strange face on his territory, especially if that face recurred.

'Who you ought to see,' he said, 'is Rupert. Rupert knows every face as passes.'

'Who's Rupert, and where can I find him?'

'He works for the Cleaning Department. You'll usually find him along here this time of day, sweeping up. Been doing it for years. You know, with a barrow.'

'Yes, I know the Cleaning Department's barrows. Where will I find Rupert?'

'He'll be here. . . .'

'I don't have much time. . . .'

'Then come back in the morning. He always takes his morning cup of tea at the Silbertoft Grill down there. Every morning at nine o'clock, regular as clockwork.'

'You don't know where he might be now?'

He chuckled. 'Would you believe it; he's finished early tonight. It's his big night. He belongs to a club. Very special. Men who escaped from certain death by parachute. In the last war. They have a reunion every year to talk over old times. Rupert was telling me this morning. Apparently they never let him put his hand in his pocket and he winds up paralytic drunk. Yes, I should come back in the morning if you're in such a hurry now, and have a word with Rupert. But I'd let him get his cup of tea down him first.'

Another five minutes wasted. Perhaps Rupert would have something more fascinating to talk about in the morning, when he read the papers. If I didn't quickly find Peckham Pete.

I thanked him and got back into the car. He walked across and stood by the open window. 'You might buy a paper,' he said. 'Nothing is for nothing in this hard world.'

Round the streets once more, conscious that the time was dribbling away slowly through my fingers and I had nothing to show for it. Each time I returned to the back of the hotel, each time I set off down yet another road the two of them could have walked. Too many variations, too many combinations of left turn right turn. For all I knew their destination could be anywhere within miles. I shunned the main road since all the derelict houses along it had been pulled down; apart from Arlington Station there was no waste ground. I drove on to the station. It had been a Builder's Merchants' offloading point in the days before pallets and road transport. Once it had businessmen going to the City before they moved out to Esher or started using taxis. Once the sand and gravel quarry had been active but that had been boarded up since I had been a copper. I drove around the station, just in case, but could see no trace of anyone or sign of anything unusual.

I had just come out of the station when I saw another newspaper-seller. This one had an elaborate stand with magazines and a few books on display. The woman running it was wearing a heavy overcoat and a black apron over a woollen dress, and though the day was not particularly cold she wore a knitted balaclava helmet and a man's trilby hat on top of that. I asked her my questions.

'Lor, luvaduck, lovey, I never see nothing here!' She had a jolly laugh which trembled the mountain of her body. 'If I spent my time looking around, I'd never sell nobody nothing, now would I?'

Despite her words she had seen the man from fifty yards away who bought the *Standard* she had folded for him. I persisted. I could see that, in common with many city people, she didn't like being asked questions about other people, had a natural distrust of being asked to be an informer, no matter how innocent the information. I described Bishop again, told her what little I knew about Pete. Her customers streamed past and I could not speak one continuous sentence to her without an interruption. She seemed, however, to be able to listen to me and chat to the customers simultaneously, maintaining a steady stream of that bubbling laughter. When she spoke to me, her words were wedged in between the words for other people, like a string of sausage meat that every so often is nipped off and twisted to make another link.

'No, love, as I recall – evening Harry, how's the missis – nobody like that ever buys – so you came up again, lucky bugger,

I thought you'd have a box of chocolates or something – all sorts come past here, but a couple like you're talking about – sorry, love, the *Mechanics' World* isn't in yet, how about the *Knitters' Gazette*?' – monstrous belch of laughter – 'I would remember a couple like that, but I ought to wear glasses – wholesaler's been, you'll have your *Yachting Monthly* starting next week, then we can run away on that boat of yours – tell you what, come back when the rush is over and I can sit down and think a bit – you never come for your *Spectator*, but I've saved it, wait a minute, it's here somewhere – yes, a bit later on love, we'll have time to sit down and think. It seems to ring a bell somewhere – Sorry, miss, no more *Petticoats*. Next week. Snotty bitch. I know who might help, hang on a bit and I'll get him – Fred –'

She bundled an improbable *Gardener's World* and *Evening News* combination for a woman she had spotted on the step of a bus. 'Fred,' she screeched. A small man wearing a bowler hat came out of a café ten yards from the newspaper stand with a half eaten pie in his hand.

'What do you want?' he shouted back.

'Never you mind what I want, stop stuffing your face and come over here.'

He came reluctantly across the pavement.

'This gentleman here,' she said, 'wants to know about a couple of friends of his.'

'He's not a gentleman,' he said, 'haven't you got no eyes in your head. He's a dick.'

'Tom, Dick or Harry, I don't care,' she said, bursting into laughter again. 'You've got eyes like a ferret.' She turned to me and knocked my chest as if testing me for tuberculosis. 'He can tell from two hundred yards when a girl's got no knickers on.'

Fred, with the bowler hat and a worldlywise leer on his face, with eyes like a ferret and a mind like a camera, had seen them. ' "Laurel and Hardy" I call them. Big burly lad, he's Hardy. Little old fellow, that's Stan Laurel to a T.'

It was true, when you came to think of it. Jim Bishop, Stan Laurel to perfection, the same lugubrious air, the same emaciated features.

'Always arguing, those two are, and the little fellow's laying down the law, if you'll pardon the expression. Actually,' he said, 'come to think of it, give you a better example. Ever go to the pictures? Well, you don't need to, see them all on television I suppose, re-run movies, her and me we could sit up all night watching them. Remember that *Mice and Men*, big fellow always on about rabbits? That's the young one and the other fellow always worriting away. That's him. Now I come to think of it, something wrong with his hands and his face, like he's got a skin disease.'

A positive identification is like manna from heaven to a policeman. 'That's it,' I said, 'that's them. Where do they go?'

'Always the same place, though I don't know why. There's nothing there anymore.'

'Where?'

'Is there anything in it? I mean, do I get a drink out of it?'

'Shut your gob, you greedy bugger,' the woman said, 'and tell the gentleman what he wants to know.'

'I was only asking. They go into the station. I had a bit of a laugh with them one day. I told 'em, "Last train's gone you know, went five years ago!" Well, you've got to have a bit of a laugh, haven't you? Want to buy a book? It's all clean stuff. What about this one? *Return of the Werewolf*. That'll keep you awake at night.'

'I don't have any trouble sleeping,' I said to him.

I got back into the car. He came over and rapped on the window. 'Parking here,' he said, 'it's illegal. You're lucky there's no coppers about.'

The woman went into peals of laughter. 'That tongue of yours, Fred,' she said, 'it'll be the death of us one of these days.'

The railway station. Of course! I kicked myself.

Once Arlington Station had been a busy commercial place but now, as I drove in through the gate on the right, I saw the derelict waiting room. The windows had all been broken and the roof hung down at one corner, tiles slipping off it like playing cards hastily discarded. Nowhere anyone could hide. In front of me were the branch lines and sidings that had been used by builder's merchants, now a mass of heaps of broken brickwork and torn bags of hardened cement. Beyond them was what had been the coal sidings, bays of railway sleepers piled end on end covered in rainwashed slack. There'd been talk for years of building a conference centre and exhibition hall on this site, but like so many long-term plans, it had not progressed beyond the drawing board. The yard was a forest of lupins and angels hair; the yellow spikes of golden rod rippled in the evening breeze, asserting their van Gogh beauty through the London grime. It was a paradise for cats, a landscape like those of the war artists who painted Berlin after the bombing, finding natural beauty in the detritus of man's existence.

I drove the car past the former coal sidings, moving slowly, eyes looking everywhere. The only souvenirs of human habitation lay in the broken artifacts, a rusted bedstead, a car without roof or doors, a pram that had carried a platoon of children. The quarry was at the far end. I cursed myself for not having thought of it sooner. Once, as a copper, I'd followed a man in there, a drunken Yorkshireman who'd picked up an iron bar and yelled alcoholic defiance. He'd killed three people since he'd left the pub and didn't care if I was the fourth. They gave me a new helmet but I kept the old one dented as a souvenir. Shortly after that they boarded the entrance with old sleepers from the coal yard, covered in corrugated iron.

I stopped the car, turned off the engine, and eased the door open. When I stepped out the ground beneath my feet was slimy with the sooted grease of years. I buttoned my coat about me, cursing when I remembered it was my best green-checked sports jacket and Sarah had protested when I had put it on that morning. I'd been in a hurry, grasped the first jacket I saw in my meagre wardrobe. They give us a clothing allowance but it isn't enough to keep us in ties.

The corrugated iron across the entrance to the quarry had been lifted. Two railway sleepers had been pulled aside. You could drive a car in there. A Sparkling Cleaning Company van. There were tyre treads on the ground. Two sets. Presumably one in and one out.

I waited for a moment and listened. All about me the traffic of London rumbled but here I was in a quiet oasis. It was hard to believe I was in the centre of one of the oldest cities in Europe. Once these had been fields and to ride out here on horseback was an adventure. I heard a pigeon to my left, felt the rustle as two dozen or more Cockney sparrows fled from a bush at my approach. The evening mist was coming down, dank and cold and carrying with it the dust and soot of the skies above me, the blanket that envelops a city like a clammy hand.

I moved cautiously to the left of the gate through a shrubbery of waist-high weeds, careful to avoid the rusted tin cans, the oily car parts, the sodden paper that nourished their roots. The quarry lay to my right, a dimple in the ground like a woman's navel. I could not see into it and therefore presumably could not be seen by anyone inside. It was about a hundred feet long, fifty feet wide and, as I remembered, about thirty feet deep in the centre. The walls were sheer and covered in vegetation which disguised the fact that for years the hole in the ground had been used as a tip. A car could drive into the bottom of it and drive out again. In Victorian times someone must have thought he'd stumbled on a fortune when he dug in his shovel and came out with gravel, but it had turned out to be a phantasy, a geological abnormality. The gravel had run out almost as soon as they started to dig it and all that was left was a rocky hole in the ground.

I looked down at my trousers. Sarah had complained when I put them on too since I'd bought them only a month ago. I dropped to my knees and started to crawl through the sheaves of golden rod. Within moments I was wet through and my hands were covered in grime and grease. The shaking flower heads dropped pollen on my face and I felt a terrible urge to sneeze, but I held it back, crawling steadily forward. Suddenly my right knee slipped and I sprawled full length on the undergrowth. A dog had been this way too, leaving traces of his passage. I had no time to clean it off. I slid forward an inch at a time till I reached the edge of the cleft. Down below me the quarry spread, a scar in the ground, its sheer sides livid with foxgloves and willow-herb. In the bottom of the quarry, all of which I could see from where I was lying, were two rusted cars, a motor bicycle without a front wheel, a large refrigerator on its back with its door off, and a hut.

The door of the hut was open about twelve inches.

Two pigeons were sitting on the roof; another flew down to join them, walking about to select a squatting place.

A large black and white cat, fifteen feet from the hut, watched the pigeons, its head moving from side to side. It crouched flat to the ground and crawled slowly forward in the stupid ostrich-like way that cats have, thinking themselves invisible. I watched the cat slowly draw near the hut, then tense itself to spring. Suddenly, though I could see no reason for it from that distance, the cat leapt into the air screeching, turned round and fled into a nearby thicket of brambles.

I was convinced that someone, sitting in the hut behind that partly open door, had flung a stone at it. I looked at the hut for other signs of movement but could see nothing. You develop a sixth sense. You go into a room at night or a dark alleyway. Once I went into a theatre. You stand still, hear nothing, see nothing, and yet the hair prickles at the back of your neck. You know someone is there; just as I knew someone was in that hut.

That someone could have a shotgun pointing out of that open doorway.

There was no way into that quarry, no route anyone could take without being seen by someone sitting in that hut in that open doorway.

I crawled backwards, this time avoiding the path of the dog, though I snagged my knee on an old car bumper and felt the cloth tear. I got to the car and switched on the radio, waiting from habit for it to warm up even though I knew the transistors didn't need it.

They put me on to Jock.

'Let me talk to the chief superintendent,' I said.

'You have to be joking. He's breathing fire in here, wanting to know where you are. We've been calling on your radio for the last ten minutes but you've been off station.'

'Let me talk to him, Jock, quick!'

'It's your funeral.' I heard him shout, 'I have Inspector Armstrong, Chief Superintendent.' In the background I heard Pope's voice bellow 'Put him on.' It's hard to describe the venom and anger he got into those three words.

'Where the devil have you been?' his voice growled at me.

'I think I know where Prince Charles is,' I said quickly.

'That makes two of us. *I think* he's on a yacht in the mouth of the Thames. *I think* he's got his feet up reading a yachting book, glad for once in his life to be away from it all. What's *your* theory?'

'I think he's in Arlington Station.'

'Waiting for the six five special.'

Another voice broke in, and I knew that Jock, damn him, had hooked me into the network. 'Commissioner here. Why do you think Prince Charles is at Arlington Station, Inspector? If memory serves me right, that station is derelict.'

'Yes Sir,' I said, 'it is.'

It's one thing to discuss your theories man to man across a desk in the inspector's room. We do a lot of that. What about if . . . But to broadcast across a network that for all I knew could end up in a private study in Buckingham Palace, with the whole Red Alert emergency services of the Metropolitan Police Force listening, was something different. I marshalled my thoughts as best as I could. My God, what did I have other than a private conviction . . . ?

'I got a positive identification, Sir, on Bishop. He does have an intimate associate known as Peckham Pete. He has been seen going with Peckham Pete into Arlington Station. I got a positive statement from a reliable source that Peckham Pete has been seen in possession of a shotgun. I have looked into a quarry in the back of Arlington Station and I'm convinced that Peckham Pete is hiding in a shed there.'

It was thin and I knew it. Pope saw the flaw immediately.

'Why are you *convinced*, Inspector? What is the *factual* evidence? Did you see someone in the hut? Did you identify this Peckham Pete?' His voice ground remorselessly and unmercifully on.

Another voice broke into the network. A clipped Scottish voice I had not previously heard. 'Sergeant Dunoon. Records. No listing for a Peckham Pete.'

We really did have the whole of the Red Alert team on, including the newly computerized Identification Section. If Peckham Pete had been any of the pseudonyms of a known criminal the high-speed printer would already have delivered a complete biography ready to punch out down the line to any office in the country equipped with a machine. I knew for sure the commissioner would have one. I knew also the Map Section would have a large scale of Arlington Station, containing details of the quarry, even of the hut. I speculated about broadcasting my bedtime story, 'The cat and the pigeon'. Sometimes you take a chance. In my case recently 'sometimes' seems to come far too often. I told them, omitting the bit about the dog shit. My narrative was followed by one of those silences that second-rate comics performing in provincial music halls must dread, a silence so profound, so deep, I could imagine I was the only man left alive on earth.

Then the commissioner cleared his throat.

You don't get to be a chief superintendent by listening to day dreams and fairy stories.

'I don't think we should allow ourselves to be distracted from the major point of this issue at the moment,' Pope said, dismissing me by ignoring me totally. 'In five minutes time we reach the deadline this man Bishop has announced for the payment of one million pounds. We have the money here, as you know. We have not yet been able to make contact with Prince Charles, as you know. We have not been able to get any positive identification on Prince Charles subsequent to the routine telephone message from his detective reporting that they were leaving for Chatham in accordance with Prince Charles's programme for today. We know Lord Wentworth's yacht departed from its mooring on time. We know Prince Charles's car is still in the garage but that Lord Wentworth's Rolls is in the car park of the yacht club. We know Lord Wentworth gave his chauffeur the day off today. We know that an ashtray has been used in the back of that Rolls and though Prince Charles does not smoke the detective does. We have not been able to get a positive identification of the car or its passengers from any of the Traffic Divisions between here and Chatham, and we are not able to locate the vessel at sea because of ground mist and fog. We are not able to speak to them by radio but we know that the transmitter has had a fault on it and though this fault has been repaired, all our electronics experts verify that the fault could be recurrent. Returning to Bishop, we know he works for the Sparkling Cleaning Company and that this morning he took a van out of their yard at the usual time of five o'clock. He fulfilled a cleaning contract in the premises of J. P. Little and Company and subsequently another contract at the house we believe to be owned by Lord Popham in which Lord Popham keeps his own personal apartments. We know Prince Charles and his detective spent the night as the guests of Lord Popham and were seen this morning to leave on schedule. We know that Bishop was somewhere on those premises at that time and that he could have seen Prince Charles and the detective and could therefore know the nature and colour of the clothing Prince Charles was wearing. I submit that Bishop did see what I have said, did overhear a conversation which gave him reason to believe that Prince Charles would be incommunicado for the rest of this day. I believe that Bishop, with the cunning born of madness, that madness caused by his regrettable treatment as a prisoner of war, concocted this scheme in the hope of laying his hands on a considerable sum of money.'

'Thank you, Chief Superintendent,' the voice of the commissioner said, 'that was a very precise summary of the evidence we have been able to gather in the course of this long and trying day. Inspector Armstrong, if you're still there, you're the one who knows this man Bishop the best. Can you add anything to what the chief superintendent has said?'

It was a concise summary. It was strictly accurate. It lacked only one thing. My personal conviction that Bishop was telling the truth, my strong, strong – extra-sensory perception if you like to call it that – that Peckham Pete was sitting in that shed at this moment with a shotgun cradled on his knees and that in order to gain a life of ease and wealth for himself he was prepared to carry out Bishop's plan. What I had to ask myself was, if Bishop's plan failed, if Bishop didn't turn up in that quarry with those two suitcases of money, would Peckham Pete be prepared to pull the trigger on that gun? I had proved to my own satisfaction that Sir William and Dr Gervis had been wrong when they had said that Bishop was a loner. I'd established a connection, hadn't I, between Bishop and Peckham Pete? Only one thing stuck in my mind. I didn't believe that Bishop would so far trust any other individual as to leave the whole scheme at his mercy. After all, if Peckham Pete reneged on him, if he just got up and walked away from that shed, where would that leave Bishop? Bishop had been so confident. Also, what if the detective, by his trained ingenuity, had been able to overpower Peckham Pete? That one thought still niggled in my mind. But even that thought was dismissed when the next voice came on the network.

'Clark here, Ministry of Public Works. I don't know if this is relevant or if it's the right time to interrupt, but here's a funny thing. That place Arlington Station. The quarry at the back of it. I have the ground survey here, and the planning projection. Reason why the development hasn't taken place is because there are a couple of blow holes under the ground. Those blow holes, they're tidal!'

There it was, the answer to the one question that still niggled me. We'd been right in one thing all along, of that I was convinced. Friendship may go so far, one man's dependence on another, but trust is something different. I'd been right when I thought that Bishop wouldn't trust any other man in this scheme that had come to him. Pope was right in his summary, of course; the whole enterprise had come as a quick flash. Peckham Pete had been riding in the Sparkling Cleaning van. Bishop had overheard the conversation that told him Prince Charles would be incommunicado for the day; that's when he decided on his scheme. But here is where Pope and I disagreed. I believed that Bishop had actually carried out the kidnapping.

Another voice came on the network and I thought I recognized it, but the clipped tone spoke too briefly for me to make a positive identification.

'We think Plan A, Commissioner!' the voice said. Even those few words revealed it was not a voice you'd argue with.

'Plan A it is,' the commissioner said. 'Right, we all know what to do and we'd better make it quick. We have only three minutes left. By the way Chief Superintendent, is Bishop wearing a watch?'

'No, Commissioner, but there's a clock outside his cell door.'

'That was an oversight. Okay everyone, Plan A.'

I knew Plan A would be to give the money and then follow Bishop by electronic and leapfrog surveillance.

'Commissioner,' I said, knowing that Pope would hate me for going over his head. 'May I suggest one thing. I'm thinking about something Sir William said about the effect on other would-be kidnappers when it gets out, as inevitably it must, that this payment has been made. I'm thinking of the collective security of every individual in this country who comes into the public eye.'

'What's your suggestion, Inspector? Your other point is taken.'

'That the money be handed over to Bishop in Arlington Quarry, after a search has been made of those blow holes.'

'You don't give up, do you, Inspector?' Chief Superintendent Pope growled. I waited in the tense silence that followed, knowing they'd be using the other line for consultation, to get a decision I knew would be final.

'Very well, Inspector Armstrong, we'll do that. It is preferable, anyway, to hand over the money off police premises. Apart from anything else, it will give our surveillance a better start. Has everybody understood that?' the commissioner asked. 'It's still Plan A, but we move the centre of the matrix to Arlington Station.'

There was a chorus of 'yesses' down the line. I hadn't realized how many people were involved.

'Just one more thing, Commissioner,' I said. 'Could Bishop not be told where the hand-over point is located, and can he be brought here in a closed van so that he can't see where he's coming to?'

'Yes, we'll do that. You have that, Transport Five?' the commissioner said. Transport Five said they had.

Pope had to have the last word. 'And you, Inspector Armstrong, stay out of that quarry until I get there.'

I switched off the radio to avoid acknowledging.

CHAPTER ELEVEN

I sat in the Ford Escort and waited for the first car. They arrived within a couple of minutes. They knew nothing of what was going on, but the signal that sent them had instructed them to place themselves at my disposal pending the arrival of the Incidents Officer, Chief Superintendent Arthur Pope.

I gave them rapid instructions, saw the second and third cars arriving and posted them at each end of the station with a 'nobody in, nobody out' instruction. Then I crawled back to the lip of the quarry but this time near to the entrance ramp. I looked down. The light was just starting to go, but everything was bathed in that pre-dusk radiance that emphasizes the outlines of buildings. I looked at my watch. The deadline was past, two minutes ago. Did Peckham Pete have a watch? How would he know when the deadline came? And, on which deadline had Bishop instructed him to move? Assuming Peckham Pete was in the shed. I refused to let my mind think what would happen should the building turn out to be empty, or occupied by a tramp. By asking for the handover to take place in the quarry, I'd really gone out on a limb. Chief Superintendent Arthur Pope was just the man to saw it off, to send me crashing down without mercy.

The foxgloves, and the willow herb were still. Helen was interested in that sort of thing; once I'd bought her a couple of books and whenever we went for a walk, she'd identify all the plants we'd see. My heart was full of relief that she was safe again. Somehow, I'd make it up to Sarah that she'd had to suffer with the kid all alone. At least I told myself I'd make it up, but how can you? My mind free-wheeled. I'd take Nancy and Sarah out together, see if they got on together. Have Nancy's boy over, let him meet my boy, Thomas. Thomas would smarten him up a bit.

The cat was back. Still after the pigeons. Cats are stupid animals. He was approaching down the same route. He'd learned nothing. His head flicked backwards and forwards, and now I saw the door of the hut open slowly, wider. I felt a shock thrill of excitement run through me. No wind, was there, if the willow herb was still? No wind to blow that door further open, was there? The door went wider and wider, slowly, so slowly. The cat crawled forwards, belly to the ground, head floating side to side like one of those animals idiot people put on the back windows of motor cars.

I saw him. His bulk filled the doorway, seemed to ooze forward out of the murk. The newspaper-seller had been right. Laurel and Hardy! Big, bulky, no more than a boy, and in his hands not a shotgun but a catapult. He levelled the catapult, pulled back the saddle, and let go. This time he scored a direct hit and the cat yowped six feet in the air before it came down like a cartoon animal, its legs already cycling as it hit the ground and took off.

A *catapult*! I scrabbled right, towards the ramp into the quarry. A constable from one of the cars was standing there, and I raised my hand and put a finger to my lips to warn him to make no noise. He understood. I crawled back to the edge. Peckham Pete must have gone back into the hut because the door was nearly closed. It opened again and he stood there and this time it wasn't a catapult he was holding in his hands. This time, it was a shotgun. Double-barrelled, broken open. He looked at the breech and, satisfied, snapped the gun closed. Two barrels, side by side. No doubt each one loaded.

He cradled the gun under his arm, lifted his wrist and looked at his watch. Then he began walking determinedly across the quarry. I didn't stop to think. At moments like that, you either think and do nothing or you act instinctively. I leaped down onto the ramp and walked rapidly forward.

'Pete,' I shouted, 'Peter.'

He stopped and turned and the shotgun was coming up. He reached his left hand across and grasped the barrel. His right hand dropped to the stock and he was holding the shotgun at his side. The barrels were pointing straight at me, but I shouted again, walking quickly forward, 'Peter. Jim Bishop sent me. Jim Bishop and Megan Davies.'

The names got through to him. The gun was still pointing at me, but his stance had relaxed. He was still suspicious but prepared to listen.

'Jim Bishop has sent me,' I said, 'and Megan Davies. It's all off. It's all off.'

'It's all off . . .?'

'Yes.'

'Who are you?' Gun up, grip firm again.

Take a chance, a million small chances that add up to one large chance. 'I was in on it from the start. I set it up. But now it's all off.'

Eight feet from him. Danger spot. Too far to dive at him, and so near I'd get the blast of both barrels. Don't show fear, they say, but how do you do that? Smile at him, for God's sake smile at him. Big lad, might be puppy fat but God, how much of it there is. Blond hair like straw, start of a stubble on his chin, fuzz on his side cheeks, a desperate attempt to grow a beard. Wearing a jeans jacket and jeans trousers and a pair of those vivid orange yellow boots with thick crepe soles. T-shirt under the jacket as black as the dirt beneath his fingernails. Smudges across his face. Thick lips, wet. Eyes set too close together in that fat face.

'It's all off?' he asked. His voice was slow and heavy and had a west country burr to it. He looked like a farmhand come up to the big city, an innocent abroad. Cautious, country cautious. I looked at his hand clasped around the barrel of the shotgun. His fingers were stained brown and yellow. Move forward slowly. My stomach already felt as if the hole had been blown in it.

'Give us a cigarette,' I said.

Instinctively his hand left the barrel of the gun and went up to the pocket of his jeans jacket but then he remembered.

'I've smoked 'em all,' he said. 'I hoped you might have some.'

I took another pace forward slightly to the side, put out my hand, touched the cold barrel of the gun. 'That's a nice one,' I said. 'I've always wanted one like that. Can I have a look?'

It wasn't all puppy fat and the barrel didn't waver as I tried to pull it towards me. 'No, you can't,' he said. 'It's mine!'

'Megan told me about it. I've never seen that kind before.'

'She tried to take it away. Never seen one of these? Ah, very common where I come from. Shooting these before we come out of the pram. Nothing gets away when I got this in my hand. Rabbits, hares. I couldn't tell you how many pheasants I've brought down!'

'Ever tried for a moorhen?'

'Ah, that's shooting. Up and over you get anything, but a moorhen, like snipe, dodgy buggers, flying low, allus away. That's shooting.'

'I can see you know what you're doing.' I knew what *I* was doing! I'd moved to the side and the shotgun was pointing past me. He was a big farm lad and it wasn't puppy fat. I could see that from close up. It'd be a lucky hit that would knock *him* down.

'Jim Bishop told me about the water. Sounds interesting.'

'Oh, you like that, do you?'

He walked across the quarry and I followed him, searching the ground for something that would help. Good as he undoubtedly was with that gun I'd only have a chance for one go at him. I'd never get a second chance. We stopped at a point halfway across the quarry where a big paving slab was lying on the ground. He nodded to it. 'Pick it up,' he said.

I looked at it. 'On my own?'

'Why not? Bishop can shift it. I can't let go of this gun. You don't want me to put it down in this filth?'

I took a corner of the paving stone and heaved, managed to get it on edge and dropped it over at its back. The hole it revealed was a rough circle two feet in diameter. He crouched down. 'Now!' I thought, but it was too risky.

'Halloooo,' he shouted down the hole and his voice came back as a ghostly echoing reverberation. 'How do you like that?' he said. 'Never heard nothing like that, have you?'

I never had. The sound tingled my nerve ends but I waited. There was no reply. I looked down into the hole but could see nothing.

'Go get that brick,' Pete said. I did as he told me, humouring him, and dropped the brick down the hole. The splash it made boomed and rolled around inside.

'It's better early in the morning,' he said. 'The water is a lot lower down then.'

He stood up across the hole from me, the shotgun still firmly held in his right hand with his fingers through the trigger guard.

'I wish you'd turn that thing away,' I said, 'I'm nervous of guns.'

He laughed. 'You're the same as Jim,' he said. 'He's nervous of guns. A gun in your hand makes you the top man. There's nothing like a gun!'

'That's what you and Bishop used to row about, isn't it?'

'Well, sometimes he made me sick, letting himself be pushed around!'

'Is this the best hole?' I asked casually.

'Oh no, the other one is better.' My heart skipped a beat.

'Shall we drop stones down the other one?'

'You crazy or something? You know what Bishop said.'

'Oh yes, it'd be dangerous to drop stones down there, wouldn't it?'

He laughed. 'That's a good one,' he said, 'dangerous! That's a good one. When's Bishop coming?'

'I suppose he'll be here any minute.' I picked up another brick and had edged round to the side of him. When I said Bishop would be coming soon, instinctively he turned to look at the entrance. The brick hit him on the hard bone behind his ear and, as he fell slowly down, I reached over him and grasped the shotgun. Some residual force remained in his fingers, causing it to twitch. Both barrels of the shotgun exploded and the boom echoed around the quarry. Pellets spattered into the earth four feet in front of us and whizzed off the flat ground, but by then I had yanked the gun out of his nerveless fingers and stepped back from him. He wasn't going to move for some time.

'Inspector Armstrong. Come out of there *now*! Fast!' The voice of Chief Superintendent Pope echoed over the quarry and I raced back up the ramp.

The commissioner got out of his car which had obviously just arrived. I knew his face well, that iron grey hair under his flat peaked hat. I saw the plain van from our Division and knew that would be where they were holding Bishop. There were five police cars and a police ambulance, a Fire Department tender, a Royal Navy mini-bus in which three men were already wearing frogmen's suits. So the commissioner, at least, had taken me seriously.

'I told you to stay out of that quarry,' Pope said.

'There are two of those blow holes. They're in the other one.'

'Where is it?' the commissioner said quickly.

'I don't know but it won't be hard to find.'

'Don't let's waste time.' As he turned round and started to wave his arms I saw the Rolls Royce come into view, its front pennant waving. So *they* had taken me seriously, too.

The commissioner beckoned to the frogmen and policemen started to climb out of the cars.

'Line abreast,' Chief Superintendent Pope shouted, 'and slowly forward.' There was no confusion as we prepared to go.

'You and you,' Pope said, pointing to a sergeant and a constable, 'go and get that lad. From the way Inspector Armstrong hit him with that brick I don't think you'll have any problems.'

The driver climbed out of the commissioner's car.

'A message for you, Commissioner,' he shouted.

'Hold it a minute,' the commissioner said to Chief Superintendent Pope, as he went to stand by his car. 'Turn it up,' he said to the driver who wound the loudspeaker to full volume. The commissioner took the microphone. 'Commissioner here,' he said.

The voice that came on the loudspeaker was shatteringly familiar. I'd heard it on radio and television several times. I'd been one of the men drafted to the Investiture in Wales. I'd guarded him at the many public functions he'd attended on our patch.

'They tell me you've been looking for me, Commissioner,' he said.

Everyone was now looking at me, including the commissioner.

'I'm afraid the radio's been giving us a spot of bother but it's all right. We've got it fixed now. Was it anything important?'

The commissioner pressed the button on his microphone. He could have been pressing my windpipe. 'No, Sir,' he said, 'it's nothing important, nothing at all in fact.' He slowly put the microphone back into the hands of his driver.

The moment was frozen in time.

I looked about me at the men poised ready to go into the quarry, the navy frogmen, the ambulance, the squad cars, the car with the pennant fluttering over the bonnet, and finally the plain van in which sat a man and a million pounds, a man I'd allowed to take me on the biggest con I'd ever known.

'You blasted, blithering, stupid, ridiculous . . .'

The commissioner put his hand on Chief Superintendent Pope's arm. 'Don't say another word, Arthur,' he said, 'you could use up the whole dictionary and not do justice to the way we feel. Inspector Armstrong,' he said, turning to me, 'I'd like you to report to your chief inspector, and after that you can report to Chief Superintendent Pope. Last of all, you can report to me.' He waved his arms and everyone went back to their cars as if sucked there by a vacuum.

I walked across to the back of the plain van and flung it open. Bishop had heard every word and knew the game was up.

'You made all this up,' I said.

He smiled at me.

I reached in and grabbed him by the shoulder. 'You made all this up,' I said. 'You were sweeping the stairs when Prince Charles and his detective came down, you heard them say something about going out on a yacht and the radio being on the blink – you knew they'd be out of touch all day and so you made it up.' I pounded his shoulder. 'You came into the station, you bastard, and you found *me* and you made it up, you made it all up!'

There was a red haze of anger in front of my eyes and I swear that if they hadn't pulled me off him I would have killed him but they dragged me off him and the last I saw as they slammed the door was his face smiling out at me, the scarred, twisted, malevolent face of the man on whom I'd squandered so much care.

'Get that lad out of the quarry,' Pope said, 'and bring him into the station, and Armstrong, don't screw that up! For God's sake, don't screw that up!'

The cars had started already to pull out of the yard and I stood immobile until they had all gone, including the one with the pennant flying above the bonnet. I turned and walked back down the ramp into the quarry. Pete was still unconscious. I bent over him and looked at the back of his head where the brick had hit him. I lifted one of his eyelids. Thank God he wasn't dead.

A lonely old man, and a confused young boy, the unlikely

combination of Jim Bishop and Peckham Pete. A Laurel and Hardy of loneliness. Society as we know it, civilization as we call it, has no room for men like Jim Bishop and Peckham Pete except on its own terms. Peckham Pete I thought. We hadn't even got his name right. He should have been Dorset Dan or Cornwall Charley. Jim Bishop and him, two nomads coming down here in this quarry as an oasis of peace in the arid desert of the city, dropping stones down the hole and waiting for the reflected sound. At least here their despair received an answer even if it was only an echo of itself. How desperate a man can become to get an answer, building up slowly over the years a force of evil hatred against those he imagines are deaf to his pleas, blind to his inner needs. How tempting to think of taking a shotgun and holding it at someone and saying 'Get into the van' and driving them to the quarry and putting them down a hole to squat like rats on some ledge of rock waiting for the water to come up and engulf them. How easy to do that in this city, where everyone has his own preoccupations. From the depth of that frustration Jim Bishop had concocted a way to get money, to give himself the peace, security and independence for which he longed. The kidnapping itself was probably quite spontaneous, without any premeditation. But when the golden opportunity had come, when he had overheard that Prince Charles was going to be incommunicado for the day, the one man for whom he thought he'd be certain to get a million pounds, the spontaneous action had come to have meaning. Only one man could tell me which had come first: the kidnapping or the idea of getting the million pounds. And that man had already conned me once. He wasn't going to con me a second time.

I walked across to the second hole and pulled back the pavement stone. I looked down into the hole and saw the face peering out at me, the face that to Bishop was synonomous with the authority he hated, the man he'd kidnapped *before* he thought of this scheme to raise a million pounds.

'You can come out now, Mr Jackson,' I said.